Chapter One

I f only he weren't so damned *attractive*!

The thought slid unbidden and unwanted into Vary's brain as she stood in the tiny room, staring helplessly at the man who had just come in, his bulk seeming to fill the dim space and making it quite impossible for her to escape. Though why she should want to, she didn't know. She had a *right* to be here, hadn't she? More than *he* had, that was for sure . . .

Swallowing the fear that rose sourly in her throat, Vary tilted back her head and tried to meet his eyes but he had his back to what little light there was, and his face was so deeply tanned that she could see only the gleam of white teeth as he spoke. Her heart was thumping raggedly, her blood roaring in her ears so that she barely heard his words, and he had to repeat them before she could take them in.

"I said, what in hell's name are you doing here?" His voice was deep, with a timbre that could, in other circumstances she guessed, caress the ears like dark brown velvet − but just now it was rasping, as rough and hard as granite. And why should she care what it sounded like at other times anyway?

Vary summoned up all her courage. She kept her hands clenched behind her back, lifted her chin again and found her voice. It was a bit wavery, she realised with disgust – but at least she could speak.

"I might just ask you that! You certainly seem to have made yourself very much at home." Her eyes took in the cheerful disorder of the room, books piled here and there, a sweater thrown carelessly over a chair, the cushions of the settee squashed by the weight of a heavy body – the body that was now looming over her so threateningly, moving closer so that she stepped back and ended her words on a squeak. "I'd like to know just how you got in."

"Through the door, how else?" He sounded almost bored now and with his change of position the light fell on his face a little, so that her fascinated gaze could take in the lean planes, the broad forehead with its hard line of black brow, the eyes that were so dark they looked like polished jet. The mouth could have been sculpted and, with those white teeth, must be able to smile with the most devastating charm – but why did she have to keep thinking like this? Vary's mind flooded again with her fears. The man was an intruder in her cousin's cottage – he could be dangerous – and the fact that he was also impossibly attractive didn't count in his favour at all.

It had never occurred to her that it wouldn't be her cousin Jeff who was occupying the cottage when she arrived. Of course, it had been several months since she had written to him to ask if she could use it during the early summer while she was on her tour of Europe. A week or two in Brittany would, she had felt, make a welcome break in her journey through Scandinavia and Germany before going on to Spain. And Jeff had written back with his usual easy-going cheerfulness, telling her that the cottage was going to be empty until he went there for his own holidays at the end of July, and she was welcome to use it for as long as she liked.

It hadn't seemed odd that when she arrived there were, after all, signs of occupation. It was Bank Holiday week in England – half-term for teachers like Jeff – and he might easily have decided to come over for a few days. She'd been delighted at the thought, and looked forward to seeing him when he returned from wherever he'd gone.

It had never struck her that it might not be Jeff who would return.

Vary looked up at the man who was now far too close for comfort. Her breathing was jerky and she was vibrantly aware of his huge masculinity. Was it just because the room of this tiny French cottage was so small, or was he really some kind of giant? She swallowed and pressed back against the wall. Whatever happened, she must remember that *she* was the one in the right. Anger was her only weapon, let him intimidate her and she was lost.

"Just who are you?" she demanded fiercely. "Who

gave you the key, or did you break in?" She hadn't noticed anything wrong with the door when she'd opened it with her own key, but that meant nothing. "What's your name?"

"I'm asking the questions." His tone was flatly uncompromising. "I happen to be a friend of the owner, and I'm staying here to do some work. He gave me the key, and I'm looking after things for him generally. So now let's have a few answers from you. How did *you* get in?"

Vary ignored that. "A friend of the owner?" she repeated sceptically. "You'll know his name, then, of course."

"Of course." He was almost pinning her against the wall now, his broad chest barely a centimetre away from the points of her breasts. "The cottage is owned by Jeff Barlow. He's a teacher in Chichester, Sussex, England." His voice was heavy with sarcasm as he reeled off the address. "Satisfied?"

Vary bit her lip. Well, that still didn't *prove* anything. He could have found out Jeff's name and occupation from something in the cottage. "I'll be satisfied when you tell me your name and Jeff confirms that you're a friend of his," she retorted. "As it happens, he's my cousin – and I don't ever recall him mentioning you."

"Since you don't know my name, that's hardly surprising. And as for you being his cousin –" the finely chiselled lips curled in a sneer "—well, you'll need to think up something better than *that*." He moved suddenly and Vary closed her eyes, panic kicking her heart, but when she opened them again he'd moved away. "All right," he said, sounding bored again. "Let's leave it at that, shall we? I can see you haven't started to rifle the place – obviously you'd only just got in. So why don't you get out, and get as far away as you can, before I call in the police? No doubt you're well known to them already – by repute if not in person."

Vary stared at him, indignation quelling all fear. Did he really, seriously mean that he thought she was a *burglar*? Did he really believe she'd forced her way in to ransack the place? She shook her head – and then remembered something.

"I may not have been here long enough to steal whatever you might have that's precious," she began, letting the scorn show in her voice and eyes as she took in the shabbiness of his denims and sweater, "but I found that door you keep locked. Just what have you got in there, Mr—" she floundered, then recovered herself – "just what have you got to hide?"

"So you *have* been looking around." His eyes narrowed with distrust and he moved towards her again. "Maybe I won't let you go quite so readily. Maybe we should talk a little more. About just what you're looking for, for instance. About how you knew where to come." He had one hand on the wall at each side of her head, trapping her there, and once again Vary was overwhelmingly aware of his nearness. Attractive she thought, looking up at the grim face – how could she have ever thought him attractive? He was nothing more than a savage! The fact that he hadn't touched her yet was of no comfort – she had a petrifying feeling that this was a man who would treat a woman as casually as he might treat a fly. And as brutally.

"Get away from me," she said, her voice trembling. "Get away. I've told you – Jeff's my cousin. I had a key. It was all arranged that I'd come here and if you know him, you'd have known that. *If* you know him."

"Well, you certainly have a nerve," he said marvelling, his breath warm on her cheek as his eyes bored into her. "Keeping up this pretence that you actually know Jeff—"

"I told you, he's my *cousin.*"

"A fact that you didn't mention until *I'd* told you his name. No, you can't fool me quite so easily, little Miss Innocent. Oh, yes, those wide brown eyes might well have got you a long way, but this is where the party stops. And before I send you on your way, I want the answers to my questions. How did you know where to come? How did you know I was here? And just who sent you?"

Vary stared at him, baffled. He just wasn't making any sense at all. Oh Jeff, she thought despairingly, is this man really a friend of yours? Is this just another one of your mix-ups? Or is there something more sinister behind his presence here? A shiver racked her body and she felt sick.

Oh God, this is it, she thought as all the warnings she'd received about travelling alone went through her mind. You're crazy, her friends had told her, taking off through Europe without a companion. Anything could

happen – and probably will. Rape . . . even murder
. . . She'd laughed at them all. She wasn't going to
hitch-hike, she'd assured them. And she'd always be
careful.

And now, here she was, in the one place which could
have been counted on to be safe, trapped by a bear of
a man who seemed to think she owed him something.
Answers he'd demanded, but if she couldn't give them
he seemed quite capable of exacting some other kind
of payment.

Vary's thoughts were an incoherent jumble, flicking
in and out of her mind like jagged darts. Uppermost
were the sensations that were scorching through her
body, sensations she had never even dreamed of and
didn't much like. A trembling somewhere low in her
stomach, a spiral of something that felt unnervingly
like excitement – like a child waiting to go to a party.
And a melting weakness in the region of her knees,
something like, but a hundred times more devastating
than, the weakness she had felt while waiting to run an
important race during the school sports.

Children's parties! School sports! What could be
less appropriate for the sensations she felt now, for
the situation she was in? Her heart kicked and she
felt a jab of pure terror. She stared up into his eyes,
unaware of how wide and dark hers were just then, as
dark as a cat's, knowing only that his were like blazing
blue sapphires.

The man dropped his arms and moved away, leaving
Vary sagging against the wall, her mind and body a

battleground of warring sensations. Her breath came raggedly, her heart was thumping almost audibly into her throat, her legs were trembling. But even as she gazed at him her mind began to clear.

Vary was no fool, nor was she totally ignorant. She was well aware of the magnetism that had hit her the first moment she had turned and seen the man in the doorway. She'd known from that moment that it was dangerous – and now she knew why: it was because there was something in her, some chemistry, that responded to it – oh, only on a purely animal level, but that made it all the worse. That she – she who had consistently refused to go to bed with any of her previous boyfriends – could react like that with a man she'd only just met and neither trusted nor liked! It was a piece of self-knowledge that she could have done without.

"Now perhaps you'll leave me alone," she said shakily, and saw one dark eyebrow rise.

"I can tell you, I'm only too pleased to comply. My life's quite complicated enough as it is." His eyes narrowed; they were a dark, almost navy blue, she saw, and not black as she'd thought at first. "All right. We'll talk. What's your name?"

Keeping a careful eye on him, Vary left the support of the wall and moved to one of the chairs. She sank into it, leaning her elbows on the table, and brushed back her long dark hair with one hand. Her face was pale in spite of its tan as she gazed up at him, and her small body was still shaking. She saw an odd quirk touch his mouth as he looked down at her, but the expression was gone before it could be identified.

"I don't see why —" she began, but his exasperated sigh cut her short.

"Don't let's start all that again. You've obviously got some purpose in coming here and I'd be interested in hearing what it is. The trumped-up one first, if you insist, but you may as well give me the truth. I'll get it in the end."

"There's *only* the truth," she said wearily. "I'm Vary Carmichael. I'm on a tour of Europe — I started in Scandinavia, went through to Germany and Switzerland and now I'm on my way through France. I knew I'd need a couple of weeks in one place at some point and Jeff said I could use his cottage. That's all there is to it."

The stranger's eyes darkened with suspicion. "Doesn't sound very likely, I'm afraid. You say you're touring Europe? Alone?"

"Yes," she said, and regretted it at once. She would have felt a good deal safer if he'd thought she had someone else with her — a big, husky boyfriend for instance.

"Hitch-hiking?"

"No — using public transport mostly: trains, buses. And walking wherever I can." She caught his expression. "And I don't sleep rough either. I stay in inns, rooms, wherever I happen to be."

"I still don't think it sounds very likely," he said. "The kind of tour you're describing takes money, however you do it. And time. How do you come to have so much of both, at your age?"

"I'm twenty-three," she said with dignity. "I've worked ever since I left school. And I do have some money behind me. Though what business that is of yours," she added belatedly, "I can't imagine."

"Maybe more than you think." His eyes were still on her, their blue the burning colour of diamonds in the sunlight. "Don't forget, I know nothing about you – and I happen to be responsible for this cottage and its contents."

"And I've only your word for that!" she retorted, recovering the anger that was her only defence against this man's arrogance. "It strikes me we'd better both keep an eye on each other until Jeff himself can clear the situation up. You haven't told me your name yet, by the way."

He inclined his head. "True. But I didn't really think you needed to know it. However, if we're to spend any amount of time here together – and I rather think we may – you'll have to have something to call me. Make it Thorne."

Vary blinked. "Thorne? You mean Mr Thorne?"

"Just Thorne," he said equably, and clearly intended to say no more. "Let's hear more about this trip of yours. Where did you intend to go after leaving here?"

What did he mean – *did*? As if her plans were coming to a sudden halt . . . Vary felt another quick leap of fear, but kept her voice steady as she replied, "I'm going on through Portugal and Spain and then making my way

10

to Italy and Greece, probably taking in Turkey as well. I haven't worked out a precise route yet."

"Quite an itinerary," he said ironically. "As you say, you definitely need money behind you. Daddy's paying, I suppose? I'm just amazed that he lets you wander the face of the earth like this. Or are you such a spoilt darling that he lets you do whatever you want, regardless of the dangers?"

Vary flinched. "I'm not a spoilt darling at all—" she began, but again he cut her short.

"Oh, come! Don't tell me the money doesn't come from your parents. You see – you can't deny it." He regarded her with a sourness that hurt. "My God," he said softly, "kids like you – you make me want to throw up. Everything you've ever wanted, handed to you on a plate, and what use are you to the world? None whatsoever – you're just parasites, the lot of you. You make me sick!"

"That isn't fair!" Vary blazed. "You know nothing about me – nothing at all! You as good as said you wouldn't believe a word I said anyway – and then you make assumptions that are nowhere near the truth. It isn't like that at all – but I wouldn't expect you to understand. And I'm not telling you any more – you'd just twist everything and turn it all into something sordid and unpleasant, and I'm not having it!" She paused, her dark eyes burning with golden fire, and blinked away the sudden tears. "And what makes you so much better than me?" she demanded. "Look at that tan – you didn't get that working down a coal mine! How dare

11

you call me a parasite when it's quite obvious you've done nothing for weeks but lie roasting your conceited male body on some Mediterranean beach. At least I've been learning – getting to know the countries and their people, improving my languages. I doubt if you've done a single thing to improve the lot of the human race."

For a moment, she feared she had gone too far. Thorne's face had darkened with every word she spoke, the heavy brows drawing together until they merged into one broad scowl of rage, the mouth tightening into a bar of steel above the rigid jaw. She could sense the tension in his body, the bunching together of muscles, the violence of the reaction that seethed below the tautly controlled surface. Her whole instinct was to cringe away, to ward off the consequences of her rash words. But Thorne did not move. There was a long, rigid silence, and then an almost imperceptible relaxation as at last he took his eyes from her face.

"You've very nearly convinced me," he said, almost absently. "At the very least, it was a clever piece of play-acting. All right, Vary, we'll leave it at that. We stay here, in our atmosphere of mutual distrust, until we can contact Jeff and get him to speak for each of us. Unless, of course, you'd like to cut your losses and depart forthwith? I'm quite willing to let you do that, provided you keep well away. Perhaps you have a cousin with a cottage somewhere in Germany?"

Vary glowered. He still didn't believe her! What he did believe, she wasn't at all sure – he seemed to have got some odd idea into his head that she'd come here to steal something – even that she'd been sent. Maybe he was just suffering from persecution mania, she thought resignedly, and wasn't that just her luck, to be shut up here with some kind of a nut just when she'd been looking forward to a couple of weeks' peace and quiet! Well, one thing was sure. She wasn't going to leave the cottage, not while he was here, not until Jeff had reassured her, anyway. There were still a few things to be explained. That locked door, for instance . . .

"I'll stay," she said coolly. "Though, of course, you'll have to open up the other bedroom. I presume you're using the large one?"

"Since you've obviously had a good look round, I imagine you know that," he replied. 'And no, I won't be unlocking the small one. Where you sleep is up to you. This small settee would be quite comfortable, I imagine – you're not very tall, are you?"

Vary gasped. He wasn't even going to offer her a bed! And she knew very well there was a perfectly good single bed in that locked room, not to mention the double that he was using. Not that she'd want to share *that* . . . Her face flamed at the thought and she saw his lips twitch maddeningly, as if he knew exactly what she was thinking.

"First come, first served," he said. "And I did under-stand from Jeff that I could rely on having *no* inter-ruptions."

"He must have forgotten," she spluttered. "It was ages ago he said I could come here. Look, I've got a key, doesn't that make you believe me? How else could I have got it?"

"And so have I. And it doesn't make *you* believe *me*. So it seems we have an impasse." Thorne watched her, then lifted his head sharply. "What's that I can smell?"

"Oh!" Vary jumped up. She'd forgotten all about the meal which she'd prepared as a surprise for Jeff when he came in. Only it hadn't been Jeff, it had been this – this *Thorne* or whoever he was – and thoughts of cooking and food had been driven right out of her head. "It's all right," she said, sinking back in her chair. "It's the *Boeuf à la Bourguignonne*. It should be ready in about half an hour – just time for me to make a salad to go with it."

Thorne's brows came together again. "*Boeuf à la Bourguignonne?*"

"Yes." She met his eyes defiantly. "I told you, I thought it was Jeff staying here. I was cooking him a meal as a surprise. Not exactly the behaviour you'd expect from an ordinary burglar," she finished sarcastically.

"Indeed not. But then, I don't think you're an ordinary burglar. Far from it." Thorne stood up and gazed down at her reflectively. "We'll each contact Jeff separately, shall we? I don't imagine either of us will trust the other to do so. And meanwhile – well, I've plenty to do. I don't know about you?"

"I expect I can find quite a lot," Vary said, wondering just what thoughts lay behind those enigmatic eyes. "I know this area quite well, you know, I've been here several times with Jeff. He's more like a brother to me than a cousin."

"Indeed." The eyes still rested on her, making her feel decidedly uncomfortable. "Then you'll be able to amuse yourself. But I think I'd rather you didn't wander too far on your own. I think, on balance, that I'd quite like to have you under my eye. Just until we know where we stand. All right?"

Vary gasped. What was he trying to tell her? That she was more or less his prisoner here? And how *dare* he assume that she would obey his impossible demands! What rights had he to order her about, to say what she must and mustn't do? None at all!

"I'll go just where I please," she told him angrily. "And I'll do what I please too. If there's anyone who needs watching, Mr – Thorne, or whatever you like to call yourself – it's you, not me. And *I'll* be doing the watching."

"Suits me," he said, and there was a gleam in his eye that Vary didn't like. "Just so long as we both stick around, it doesn't matter much who's watching who, does it?" Suddenly, to her astonishment, he laughed outright. "My God – what a ludicrous situation! I never thought I'd find myself behaving like a double agent, with all that 'he knows I know he knows' claptrap. But if that's really the way you want it . . ." He looked at her, eyes bright with laughter, but Vary refused to share the joke, whatever it was.

"Just let's contact Jeff as soon as possible and get this sorted out," she said stiffly, and his laughter faded.

"By all means." And now his tone was just a little bit *too* solemn. "And meanwhile – you've got a meal cooking out there, I understand. So maybe you'd better go and see that it's all right."

Vary got up and went out to the kitchen. She had a feeling that somehow she'd come off worst. There was something here she didn't understand – and something else, concerning his male virility and her feminine responses, that she feared she understood only too well.

And just how had she, with all her feminist instincts and determination to be no man's chattel, come to find herself out here, in the kitchen of this tiny French cottage, cooking a meal for a man she loathed? Perhaps while she was out here, on her own, she could come to terms with the situation and work out just what to do next.

Chapter Two

B ut it wasn't too easy to decide what to do next, Vary discovered as she wandered slowly along the shore ten minutes later. She dug her hands deep into the pockets of her jeans and stared at the waves that rippled over the shingly beach. Gulls swooped around her head, their screams as jagged as her disconnected thoughts. Over by the jetty a fishing boat had just tied up and its occupants were talking in loud, cheerful Breton. Vary listened automatically, but the dialect was too strong for her to follow; it was like a Londoner hearing broad Cornish for the first time.

In any case, what they were saying wasn't important – not to her. What she had to work out was just what to do about this stranger, this Thorne, who had invaded her cousin's cottage and her privacy. She had to admit, it didn't seem very likely that he would just have chosen the cottage as a squat, yet these things did happen. And if he had, it was up to her to do something about it. At the very least, she had to stay until it was confirmed that he really was a friend of Jeff's.

And if he wasn't? Wouldn't she be taking a very

dangerous risk to stay on alone in the cottage with a man of whom she knew nothing? Vary felt her flesh shiver at the thought of those dark, compelling eyes, that jutting jaw, that casual arrogance. She didn't have to remind herself that if he chose to use brute force against her, she would be helpless – her strength could never match his. Even if she were to spend the night alone with him – her heart bumped – she didn't have to let him get near her. There must be *some* way of keeping him at a distance.

If only she could use the second bedroom. But that was locked.

Vary came to the jetty and walked out along its length, nodding a greeting to the fishermen. At the end she stopped and gazed out across the gulf. Directly in front of her, she could see the island of Gavrinis, with its huge tumulus. In an area already filled with prehistoric remains, this was one of the most interesting to archaeologists and Vary had seen the excavations on one of her previous visits. She had found it strangely evocative, creeping through the low passages and trying to imagine the people who had built it and been buried there, and she had been glad to get out into the sunlight again.

The rest of the gulf was blue with dancing water. The tide was high, and the soft breeze was just enough to tease the surface into tiny white horses so that the boats moored around the little port rocked and their halyards jingled against the masts. The bay of Larmor Baden was a miniature inlet in the greater width of the

gulf; a sailor's paradise, she thought, and remembered
the fun she and Jeff had had here with the little dinghy
he used to bring across for holidays.

The familiar sights and sounds were soothing to
Vary's tumultuous feelings, and she sat down at the
end of the jetty and hugged her knees, making a
deliberate effort to relax her mind. The glittering blue
of the sea, reflecting the cloudless sky but adding its
own restless shimmer, contrasted strongly with the
green of the tree-fringed shore. Away from the village
itself, surrounding the tiny harbour, there were a few
houses along the neck of the small peninsula; around
the point, she knew, was the small island which could
be reached on foot only at low tide, welcoming visitors
but requesting quiet and peace because of the convent
that occupied its centre. And the greater part of the
gulf, dotted with more islands, large ones like the *Ile
aux Moines* and a myriad tiny, unnamed islets.

The scent of seawater and freshly landed fish came to
Vary's nostrils as she breathed deeply and remembered
some of her previous visits to this peaceful place.
Although in such a popular part of Brittany, it was
largely unknown and completely unspoilt; just a simple
fishing village, the inhabitants making a living mainly
on the oyster beds around its shores, with two or three
unpretentious hotels which attracted visitors who were
tired of the fleshpots. This was how Jeff had first
discovered it, while on holiday with his parents years
ago. He had never forgotten the few quiet days they
had spent there simply pottering about, and when he

had had an unexpected Premium Bond win a few years back he had known immediately what he wanted to do with it. "A cottage in Brittany," he'd said firmly, waving aside all suggestions of investment, new cars and so on. "What better for a French teacher? I can spend all the school holidays there and recuperate from the horrors of term-time!" And he'd given Vary that special smile and added, "It's not just for me to enjoy, either. Members of the family are welcome at any time."

That summed up their relationship exactly, Vary thought, warm gratitude flowing through her as she thought of how Jeff and his parents – her Uncle Mike and Aunt Nancy – had made her a part of their close-knit family ever since the death of her parents in an air crash eight years ago. She hadn't actually lived with them – her mother's father had taken her into his home since he lived in the same town and it had been agreed that she would be better staying in familiar surroundings. But there had never been a holiday when she had not been invited to join them, and the weekends spent at their home in the country were too many to count.

Jeff had been like an elder brother to Vary, taking the shocked, bereft teenager under his wing, having her to visit him at university, writing to her regularly, making her feel wanted, a little less alone in a suddenly hostile world; reassuring her that she still belonged. Looking back, she marvelled at his patience and understanding; only a few years older than she, he had seemed to know exactly what she was going through, exactly how to guide her gently back to acceptance and enjoyment of a life that had seemed suddenly blank and empty. It still felt empty at times – especially after Grandad had died too – but Vary never again felt quite so alone as she had during those first early weeks. Always, she knew, there were Jeff and her uncle and aunt. Especially Jeff.

She jumped and stifled a scream as a heavy hand fell on her shoulder and a deep voice said grimly, "So this is where you've got to. Contemplating your next move? Or maybe you're ready now to admit defeat and tell me the truth."

Vary jerked round. Thorne loomed over her, gigantic from this angle, and she struggled to her feet. There was no way she could meet his eyes without having to tilt back her head – he must be well over six feet – but at least she could stand straight, and the very act of tilting her head lifted her chin and made her feel better.

"I suppose you think that's clever – sneaking up behind me like that. Do you realise I could have fallen in, it's deep just here."

"No doubt you can swim," he said carelessly. "And if not, I'm quite capable of saving you. I can even administer the kiss of life." His eyes glinted as her cheeks coloured.

Vary felt her blush deepen. She resented his assumption that she was the kind of girl who slept around, and she would have liked to set the record straight. Not that it mattered a damn what he thought about her, she reminded herself fiercely. He was still distinctly suspect himself. There was as yet no proof that he'd ever met Jeff or had his permission to use the cottage, and there was still the question of that mysteriously locked room. Just what did he have to hide?

"Let's keep personalities out of this," she said coldly. "I imagine you had some reason for following me here?"

"Naturally. I wanted to keep an eye on you. As I told you earlier, I'd prefer that you didn't wander off without my knowing just where, why and for how long. Presumably you've some friends in the vicinity and I don't want you passing any little titbits of information to them."

"Look," Vary said wearily, "I've told you before, I'm on a tour through Europe – *alone*. I don't have any friends around here, other than the villagers I've got to know while I've been coming here with Jeff. I certainly don't have any plans to pass 'information' to anyone – I don't even know what information you mean." She paused, then added slowly, "But there's obviously something you're trying to hide. And I wouldn't be far wrong in guessing that it's behind that locked bedroom door. Just what is it, Mr Thorne? Just what is it you're so frightened I'll find out?"

His sapphire eyes revealed nothing. They were like glacial ice as they burned into Vary's, and she quailed but kept her own topaz gaze fixed firmly on his. The chiselled lips tightened and once again she sensed the violence of the anger that surged behind that grim expression. Vary held herself rigidly, disciplining her body not to shiver. But all he said, at last, was, "Not 'Mr Thorne'. Just Thorne will do. And now I think we'll go back, shall we? You're supposed to be in the kitchen, putting the finishing touches to that meal."

"It doesn't need any finishing touches," Vary began, but his hand was on her arm, turning her round, and his fingers were so implacably hard that she had no choice. Seething, she walked beside him along the jetty. Was there no limit to the arrogance of this man? Did he really believe he had the right to tell her where to go, and when, to keep her a virtual prisoner? Her conviction that he had never met Jeff increased. Jeff would never have let his cottage to a man like this. Never!

They walked away from the shore, through the scatter of houses that formed the village. The inn, the shop, a few cottages, some larger houses set back behind walls . . . Vary's eyes darted from side to side, hoping desperately that she might see a familiar face. But she hadn't been here for nearly three years now; even those she'd known would probably have forgotten her.

"There's a telephone!" she exclaimed. "We could ring Jeff!" As soon as she'd spoken, she wondered why she hadn't thought of it before. In one stroke, she could call Thorne's bluff and expose him for the liar she was convinced he must be. He might have learnt Jeff's name and address from something at the cottage, but he was hardly likely to have memorised his telephone number. Whereas to her, it was as familiar as her own.

Thorne stopped dead. His fingers tightened painfully on her arm and she couldn't suppress a flash of triumph in her tawny eyes as she looked up at him. Now what do you do, her eyes asked him defiantly – but to her chagrin he didn't seem in the least disconcerted.

"We certainly could ring Jeff," he agreed, "if it weren't for the fact that he's away himself on half-term holiday. Didn't he tell you?"

Vary blinked. Away? He certainly could be – she'd thought of that herself, when she'd first found the cottage occupied and thought it must be her cousin. But it might just be a clever guess on Thorne's part – he couldn't *know*. And there was one very easy way of proving it.

"No, he didn't tell me," she said shortly. "And I don't believe he told you, either. So if you don't mind I'll ring him just in case." She made for the telephone box and Thorne, his fingers still around her wrist, came with her.

"You're wasting your time," he remarked, as they squeezed into the narrow space together. "But of course, you know that, don't you. It's what you're banking on, after all." He watched amusedly as she fumbled in the pockets of her jeans. "Got the right money?"

"Of course I haven't!" An exasperation springing directly from frustration grated in her voice. "I didn't bring my bag. Have – have *you* got any?"

"Probably." He was really far too close for comfort, she thought, watching as he pushed his free hand into his own pocket. So close that she could feel every movement – and some of those movements, as he felt for his money, seemed to be unnecessarily intimate. Surely there was no need for his fingers to move against her thigh in that sensual manner . . . Her cheeks burned and she turned her head away, acutely conscious of his eyes on her face. She was wishing now that she'd never suggested telephoning Jeff – that she'd waited until later, when she could slip out alone. That was if he ever let her out of the cottage again.

"There we are. That's about right for a call to England, I should think." Thorne laid the coins on the little tray. "Now, the dialling code." He released her arm at last, not that there was any possibility of escape from this tiny space in which he had her so securely and intimately pinned, and his fingers became busy dialling. So he wasn't going to let her do the telephoning and from her position she couldn't even see what he was dialling. It could be anything!

Vary squirmed in her efforts to see just what he was doing, but her movements only made her all the more aware of their closeness. It was worse than being in bed together, she thought, and was immediately even more scorchingly conscious of him. And from his reaction, she knew he was equally aware of her. She caught his glance, resting quizzically upon her, and bit her lip. Oh God, he actually thought she was enjoying it!

"Hm," he said, his eyes still on her. "Just as I expected, no answer. Want to hear for yourself?" He held the receiver against her cheek and she heard the ringing tone, somewhere far away in England. But it was faint under the roaring of the blood in her ears, and she was too dazed to understand just what it meant. And Thorne's finger was touching her neck very, very

25

gently, so that she wanted to turn her head and lay her cheek against it.

No! He *wasn't* going to get at her like this. With a violent movement that brought her hard up against him, she twisted her head away and tried to push past him to get out. But it was useless, as she might have known it would be. The only result was that she now found herself encircled by his arms, his breath warm on her cheek, his heart beating steadily against her breast.

She wondered vaguely if he could feel her own heart, and sense the raggedness of its rhythm.

"So," he murmured, his lips almost brushing her skin, "Jeff is, as I told you, away. All right?"

"No – no, it's not all right!" If only he'd let her *go* – if only they could be outside again where the air was cool and she could get a distance between them again, remove herself from this – this – *hateful* contact. Perhaps then she'd be able to think more clearly. "You haven't proved a thing. Jeff could be out. You might not even have been ringing his number. In fact, I don't believe you were! I never saw what you were dialling – you wouldn't let me. You're lying, just as you've lied all along the line. You don't know Jeff at all, and I shall ring him myself, as soon as I get the chance, and show you up for just what you are."

"And that is?" He thrust the door open with his shoulder and stepped back into the sunlight, bringing Vary with him. Staggering a little, she ran her fingers through her hair, lifting it away from her neck to let the breeze cool her skin.

"You tell me! I just can't imagine what you're doing here – moving into someone else's cottage – keeping one of the bedroom doors locked."

"Yes," he said, staring at her. "It's that locked door that really bugs you, isn't it? And we both know why, don't we?"

"Do we?" Vary turned away as if the subject were just too tedious to go on with. "Quite frankly, I don't much care what sinister secret you're hiding behind that door. You could be Bluebeard, for all it matters to me, with half a dozen wives chopped up and packed into plastic bags. All I want is to make sure that Jeff's possessions are safe and to have a quiet break for a few days. And I can't have that with you around!"

"And the same applies to me. *I* came looking for peace and quiet too, only I want to get on with some work, not simply lie about in the sun. There's precious little chance of that with *you* about, so the sooner you stop whatever game it is you're playing and leave me in peace, the better I'll be pleased."

"Work?" Vary's brows creased. "What sort of work?"

"Never mind what sort of work. It doesn't concern you – much as you may think it does."

Another baffling statement! But Vary brushed it aside. "Are you a writer?" she demanded, remembering the typewriter that had been standing on the table. "Is that why you've come here?"

"I told you – never mind!" They were out of the village now, wandering down the twisting lane that led to the cottage, alone on its own little stretch of shore.

Vary's heart jumped as she realised once more just how isolated it was here. Her words about Bluebeard came back to her – they'd been spoken lightly enough, but suppose he did have some sinister purpose in keeping that door locked. And nobody knew that she'd come to the cottage. Even Jeff hadn't known when she'd be there. Her itinerary had been deliberately vague. And the last time she'd written to anyone had been from Switzerland.

You're being utterly crazy in going back to the cottage even for a moment, she told herself as her legs carried her closer. The only sensible thing to do is run for it – run as far and as fast as you can. But even as she thought it, she knew that it would be of no use. Thorne's legs were longer and stronger than hers. He would catch her with ease. And if he thought she might try to escape, he would make it even more difficult for her. No, the only thing to do was go back with him now, and wait for her moment.

And at the same time, she felt a curious, inexplicable reluctance to do any such thing. Why *should* she leave the cottage? she said to herself, trying to rationalise her feelings. It was Jeff's and she had more right here than anyone. There wasn't any reason why she shouldn't stay for as long as she liked, regardless of who else was in occupation.

She tried to ignore the knowledge that her reasons for staying included something else – something that was concerned directly with Thorne himself. And the strange, terrifying chemistry that sparked between them.

*   *   *

"So – how about this meal?"

Thorne closed the door behind him and the room immediately seemed smaller. The old French furniture that Jeff had bought for it seemed to crowd together, and the tiny windows let in even less light than usual. That bush wants trimming again, Vary thought randomly, and she backed away towards the kitchen.

"I should think it's ready now. I take it you won't suspect me of trying to poison you?"

His brows rose. "She goes in for sarcasm too! No, I shan't be testing it for arsenic or strychnine – I'll simply watch you taste it first. So good of you to take the trouble, after all."

"It wasn't for you," Vary reminded him tartly. "I thought Jeff was here."

"So you said." His eyes rested on her. "Well, go and dish it up or whatever you have to do. I've wasted enough time this afternoon. I don't usually bother to cook for myself – just have some bread and cheese or a meal in the village. I'll be interested to see what you can do." He didn't sound at all interested, she thought furiously, just patronising. Well, he was in for a surprise if he thought she couldn't cook – and she hurried into the kitchen, determined to pull out all the stops.

The casserole, which had been gently simmering away for several hours now, had reached perfection, and the crusty bread Vary had bought from the shop needed only a few moments in the warm oven. While it was heating through, Vary made a salad and laid the scrubbed kitchen table with the local pottery plates and dishes that went so well with the simple room. Jeff's favourite gingham cloth brightened up the rustic surrounds, and a bottle of locally made wine from his store completed the bistro effect. There was even time to slip out into the garden and collect a colourful posy of flowers to stand on the table in an old blue jug.

"It's ready," she said, and set the casserole, salad and bread on the table.

Thorne came through, looking vague as if he'd been immersed in his work and didn't really want to be disturbed. They sat down, Vary wondering just why she was doing this. Well, she wasn't really – not for Thorne. The meal had been cooked with Jeff in mind and, as she'd prepared it, she'd visualised the two of them eating it together with a lot of laughter and talk, just as usual. It was very different now, with this grim, taciturn man whom she wouldn't trust a yard further than she could throw him – but the food had been cooked and so might as well be eaten, and it might at least show him that there was something she could do. So far, he'd treated her like a four-year-old child.

Wrenching her thoughts away, she served out generous helpings of the *Boeuf à la Bourguignonne* and left him to take his own salad. The aroma of the wine-soaked beef filled the kitchen, reminding her just how hungry she was, and she took her own salad and a hunk of bread, and fell to, barely noticing Thorne's reaction. It was several moments before she realised that his expression was anything but approving.

"What's the matter?" she asked, her fork halfway to her mouth. "Don't you like it?"

"Like it?" He had eaten a good half of his plateful, she noticed, but was now looking at it as if he did indeed suspect her of trying to poison him. "Liking it doesn't really come into it. What on earth did you put into it? What in hell's name did it cost?"

"What did it cost?" Vary blinked. "I – I don't really know. There was the beef; it's good meat, it wasn't exactly cheap. And the wine, of course, and the vegetables – onions, mushrooms and so on. And the herbs, but they came from the garden. But what does it matter what it cost? The main thing is that it should taste good."

"No," he said heavily, and she stared at him in astonishment, "that is *not* the main thing. The main thing is that the human body should be fed and nourished, enough to keep it alive and healthy, not that it should be indulged and cherished and pampered with rich food it doesn't need. What you spent to make this—" he indicated the steaming casserole in front of him with a gesture of disgust "—could have fed a family for a week in some parts of the world. Don't you realise that? Or do you just never think that way? Is it perhaps that the plight of entire continents just doesn't impinge on your consciousness as you swan about Europe on your father's money?"

Vary laid down her fork. She felt almost as if she had been physically assaulted. The attack had been so unexpected it had taken her breath away. But as he continued to speak, her reeling senses recovered a little and anger began, once more, to come to her rescue.

"Now look," she said, and she was pleased to hear that her voice was barely quivering, "I don't know what's bugging you about this, but all I've done is cook a meal – a meal you seemed quite pleased to share. It wasn't cooked with you in mind, and it'll be the last meal I *do* share with you, but since it had been prepared it would've been silly not to do so this time. And what it cost is my business, I'm not asking you to contribute. But I don't see why I should be taken to task over it. The food's there in the shops, it's available and whether I use it or not isn't going to make one atom of difference to the people in the Third World, who I presume are the ones you're worrying about." She shook her head. "You know, you remind me of my father when I couldn't finish up all my dinner. 'There are a lot of little boys in India who would like to eat that', he'd tell me, and I used to want to tell him to send it out to them. I never did, of course, but I feel like that now, and I'll say it to you: if you're so worried about the Third World, Thorne – or whatever your real name is – why don't you go out there and help them, instead of preaching your sanctimonious lessons at me, when all I've done is cook you a good, but not especially elaborate, meal?"

She took a deep breath, amazed that he'd let her say so much without interruption. But at her last words his face darkened. Without another word, he pushed his plate away from him and stood up, scraping his chair back across the stone-flagged floor.

"I suppose you think that's a very clever, funny thing to say," he said, through gritted teeth. "Well, I'm afraid I don't happen to agree. All right, you've cooked the food and it would be even more stupid to waste it. But don't ever make a meal like that again, not while you're in this cottage, not while I'm anywhere around. All right?" He headed for the door, but stopped to rake her once again with his burningly dark eyes. "I live simply, on as little as I can manage," he told her forcibly, "and if you insist on sticking around, that's what you'll do too. And no more wisecracks about the Third World – or there'll be real trouble."

He disappeared, leaving Vary with the remnants of the meal strewn across the kitchen table. Bemused, still without the remotest idea of what this baffling man was all about, she lifted her fork and automatically put some more food into her mouth.

But somehow, it didn't taste at all the same. The rich, full flavour of beef, onions and mushrooms simmered for hours in red wine, had vanished. What she had on her plate now could have been nothing but ashes.

Chapter Three

Even the owls had stopped hooting by the time Vary finally fell asleep that night. Not that she had expected to sleep at all – not on that small and rather lumpy settee. It was strange how something so comfortable by day could turn into something so unwelcoming at night. Or maybe it was just the thought of Thorne, slumbering peacefully in that large double bed in the next room that was keeping her awake.

Vary twisted restlessly on the sofa. Of course, she'd never really expected that Thorne would offer her the bed, he wasn't the sort to let good manners stand in the way of his own comfort. Apart from one or two remarks about 'liberated women' he seemed not to have given it a thought. Vary was last on the scene, so she took what was left – it was as simple as that.

At least he hadn't suggested that they *share* the bed.

Sighing, Vary sat up and in the dim light from the window regarded her tumbled bedclothes hopelessly. The trouble with using a settee was that there was no way you could tuck them all in properly, so when you moved, they moved too. Which didn't matter if you fell asleep the moment you laid down your head, which was what Vary usually did. But tonight, well, tonight, tired though she was, there seemed to be no stopping the thoughts that ran like ants through her brain. And although she was normally firmly against using any artificial aids, tonight she would have welcomed a sleeping pill. Or even, she thought despairingly, a nicely judged blow with a hammer.

Once again her thoughts, like ants now settling on a juicy morsel of food, concentrated themselves on Thorne. Just what sort of a man was he? Like no one else she'd ever met, that was for sure. His face rose again in front of her sleepless eyes – darkly tanned, lean, stern yet mobile enough to express delight, fun, affection – she brought herself up sharply. How could she know that? Apart from one brief moment of laughter which she'd refused to share, she'd only seen it look disapproving; only seen those lips set in a straight, uncompromising line instead of parting in the glinting smile she imagined; only seen those eyes flashing with anger rather than deepened by desire.

Who was he, and what was he doing here? Did he really know Jeff? Was he really working? And if so – at what? Writing was the only thing Vary could think of, and she had a vague feeling that she'd heard the name Thorne before in that connection . . . but why should he be so secretive about it? Why the locked room? And why that strange reaction to the meal she'd cooked?

For the rest of the evening, they had barely spoken.

Vary had finished her own meal, more from defiance than because she really wanted it, and Thorne had disappeared into his locked room. Feeling somewhat deflated, she had spent the rest of the evening tidying up and cleaning the kitchen and living room. Thorne had been speaking the truth when he told her about his eating habits, anyway, she reflected, looking into the small fridge and the cupboards. There was very little food in the cottage; only some cheese, part of a French loaf which was now stale, some butter and staples like tea, coffee and sugar. A bowl of apples stood on the living-room table, but there was nothing else. Well, you didn't need much else if you were going to eat out every night – the inn and hotels in the village all served good meals and there were other restaurants in nearby villages. But did he sneer at their food the way he'd sneered at hers? And what was so wrong with a good meal, anyway? Did it help anyone in the Third World if Europeans deliberately starved as well?

Vary gave it up. Whoever he was, Thorne was an enigma, and one she hadn't a hope of solving, at least not without a few more clues. But she was determined that before she left here, she would know all about him. Who he was, why he was here, what he was doing.

She owed it to Jeff, if nothing else.

Dawn was colouring the sky when Vary stirred, still muffled in a confused dream in which she was convinced that there was someone in the room with her – someone who meant her no good. She struggled to call out as a shadow darkened her eyes, but her voice refused to function and she could manage no more than a strangled moan. For a moment, she thought that a hand rested as if in reassurance on her hair, and her panic subsided. And then there was the soft click of a door closing, and she came fully awake with a jump. Had it really been a dream, or had someone actually been in the room, moving about, touching her? Her mouth went dry as she jerked herself upright and stared around the room, dim with soft morning light.

There was no sound from the rest of the cottage. Outside, the birds were full into their dawn chorus, a symphony of song that must surely have drowned any small noises indoors. It must have been a dream. And yet – her eyes went to the door of Thorne's bedroom. Had he been here?

And if so, why? Had he been checking to see if she were still here? He had a curiously ambivalent attitude towards her: on one hand, he made it quite clear that she was distinctly unwelcome; on the other, he seemed to have no intention of letting her go. Vary recalled her fears of yesterday that he might not be quite sane. It seemed impossible. In any other circumstances she'd have said he was the sanest man she'd ever met. But didn't some of the craziest people seem completely sane? Some of the most brutal murderers?

Stop it, she told herself fiercely, you're just imagining things. All right, he may be a con man but that doesn't mean he's mad. Or a murderer. Not many people are, after all. And if he'd been going to do anything to you, he'd have surely done it by now.

All the same, she couldn't stay here on that settee, dressed only in the flimsy nightie she'd brought for easy carrying in her rucksack. Not now that morning was approaching. And, with one eye on the door in case Thorne should suddenly emerge, she ferreted amongst her things to find clean clothes and slipped rapidly into blue shorts and a T-shirt.

She was in the kitchen, washing at the sink, when he put in an appearance.

"Thought I heard you moving about." He leaned against the door jamb, still tousled from sleep, his shirt unbuttoned to reveal dark hairs on his broad chest. "Sleep well?"

"Perfectly, thank you." Vary had no intention of telling him about her restless night. "I don't need to ask about you, of course."

"No, you don't." He yawned a little, eyes crinkling. "It's surprising how comfortable these French beds are. I must say I think Jeff's made a good job of this little place, don't you? Comfortable without being pretentious. People who buy French cottages tend to go to one of two extremes – it's either so luxurious you're afraid to move, all the latest things brought from Paris at great expense, or it's so painfully rural it turns into a caricature. Jeff's got it just right."

"Probably because he couldn't afford to do anything else but buy what was available locally," Vary observed. "And since you admire it so much, why not ring him up and tell him so? I'll come with you." She remembered the smallness of the phone box and bit her lip, wishing she hadn't said that, but it was too late. Thorne was watching her quizzically.

"Certainly, if you'd like to. It won't be any good, of course – as I told you, Jeff's on holiday until Friday. But if you'd like to keep trying – I'm game."

"Until Friday? You never told me that."

"Didn't I? Well, I've told you now. So you see, it's only two days to wait. Unless you'd rather give it up as a bad job and move on." There was an odd glint in his eyes that Vary didn't understand, but then there was so much about this man that she didn't understand. She shrugged.

"I'll stay." She moved past him into the other room, determined to appear casual and not let him know how he affected her. "I'm just going down to the village for some croissants for breakfast," she said picking up her bag. "You won't want any, of course. Shall I see if they've got any stale bread?"

"I told you before, jokes like that aren't funny. I'll have some croissants too, and you might pick up some bread for lunch." He glanced at his watch. "It needn't take you more than twenty minutes."

Vary gasped. Was he letting her out, like a prisoner on parole? She wanted to tell him it would take her two hours if she felt like it, but it wasn't worth it. Whatever they argued about, he always came off best – and she was hungry enough to want to hurry back with those croissants. She shrugged again and went out, conscious of his eyes on her as she walked down the path.

All the same, she could ring Jeff now she was on her own. And if he were at home, he'd be certain to answer the phone at this time in the morning. Vary quickened her steps to the telephone box, and slipped inside. There was plenty of change in her bag, she knew that. Her fingers shaking with sudden excitement, she pulled out her purse and opened it.

There was, as she had thought, plenty of change inside. But that was all. Something else – something that had certainly been there yesterday – was missing.

The key. The key to the cottage. It had gone.

Vary felt her blood turn to ice. For a moment, she wondered if she could have been mistaken: put the key down somewhere indoors; left it behind. But, no. She clearly remembered dropping it back into her purse after she had opened the door on her arrival yesterday. And she'd seen it there later on, when she had checked to see if she had change for a phone call to Jeff when she'd made up her mind that she was going to do the dialling next time, just to make sure.

So Thorne *had* been in her room this morning. It hadn't all been a dream. He'd crept in while she was asleep, gone through her bag and found the key, and taken it out. It didn't take much imagination to realise why. Or why he'd been so willing to let her come out alone this morning, after saying he wanted to keep her under his eye all the time. When she returned to the cottage, complete with croissants and bread, she'd find the door locked against her. And locked against her it would stay.

Vary found she was trembling from head to foot, great long shudders that started at the nape of her neck and ran like waves down her body to her toes. It wasn't fear this time, though there was still something about Thorne that she found sinister and inexplicable. It was anger. Pure, red-hot anger. And the words that she found repeating themselves above the thunder of her blood were: He's *not* going to get away with it. He's not. He's not!

She took a deep breath. It was no use rushing back to the cottage in a rage and hurling herself at a locked door. She had to keep cool and attack the problem calmly.

And she had to ring Jeff.

As she might have known it would, the telephone rang on unanswered. Whether Thorne really knew or had just made a lucky guess, he'd been right – Jeff was away.

Until Friday, as Thorne had said? Well, she could wait until then, and maybe in the meantime she could find out a bit more about the man she was sharing the cottage with. That was if she ever got inside the door again! At the thought of her key, Vary felt her anger begin to rise once more. But she fought it down – keep calm, she said to herself – and went into the village to the *boulangerie* where she had so often shopped on previous holidays.

Perhaps the woman there would remember her and tell Thorne that she'd been here with Jeff. Vary felt a quick spurt of hope. But the stout, black-haired woman that she'd known had gone. In her place was a young girl with frizzy blonde hair, who told her that Madame Renard had gone to Marseilles to live with her son. And *non*, the girl who had helped her in those days, her niece, had gone to Paris.

Vary walked back towards the cottage, her shoulders drooping with dejection. There seemed to be no way in which she could persuade Thorne that she had a right to be here: Jeff wasn't available; there didn't seem to be anyone in the village who'd remember her. Thorne had taken her key and she had no doubt that she would find the door locked against her when she returned. And what would she do then? Little, it seemed, other than accept defeat and go on her way and find somewhere else to spend a few days before travelling on. But she was stubbornly reluctant to do that.

She had a right to be in the cottage. At least as much right – and probably a great deal more – than the enigmatic Thorne. So why should she just tamely give in and go away?

She was damned if she would!

The sea was rippling almost to the edge of the cottage garden when Vary came round the corner of the lane and, in spite of her worries, she felt the inevitable lift of her heart as she saw the feathery tamarisk and the yellow broom that fringed the rough lawn. Jeff did little actual gardening – it was impossible when he could be here for only a few weeks a year – but he arranged for a local man to keep the grass from turning to hay, and he invariably brought fresh plants for the herbs that rampaged aromatically around the kitchen door. What flowers there were, were meadow flowers and Vary was always surprised and enchanted by their variety. The wild little garden suited the cottage far better, she thought, than anything more cultivated.

She stopped to look at it for a moment. Might as well pretend, just for a little longer, that it was Jeff in there and that everything was all right. Might as well imagine that in a moment the door would open and Jeff would come out, smiling a welcome, and try to forget that it was, in fact, locked against her and that inside there were only suspicion and hostility.

And then, to her astonishment, the door did open. It wasn't Jeff who came out, it was Thorne. But he looked along the lane and saw her, and he didn't go back inside and slam the door in her face. Instead, unbelievably, he leaned against the wall and waited.

Vary approached slowly, wondering how it would be if things were different. If he could only be smiling his own welcome; holding out his arms for her to walk into . . . Angrily, she jerked her mind away from its daydreams. Why couldn't she stop thinking about him like that? All right, so he was attractive – sexy, even! But she'd known attractive men before and they hadn't made her think like this. So why couldn't she control her mind, and her body, where Thorne was concerned? She didn't even *like* him, for heaven's sake!

"Got the bread?" he greeted her laconically, and she

reflected wryly that there could hardly be a less sexy greeting than that. "Good, I'm ravenous." He ducked back inside. "I laid the little table in the garden as it's such a nice morning. Coffee's just ready."

Vary followed him inside and tipped the warm croissants into a small basket. The enticing smell of new bread filled the tiny kitchen. "If you'd eaten all your meal last night, maybe you wouldn't be so hungry now," she said tartly, and led the way back into the garden.

Thorne followed with the coffee jug. "Maybe not, but we won't go into that now. Let's start the day on a peaceful note, shall we?" He set the jug down on the rickety little garden table and smiled at her.

Vary stared at him. He really believed she'd swallow it! He really thought that if he exerted himself to be pleasant, she'd go along with him. And then what? Did he intend to kick her out straight after breakfast, still smiling that bland, and undeniably attractive, smile? Or was he going to wait until she had gone for a walk – let out again to do some shopping, perhaps – and then just quietly lock the door behind her, as she'd expected him to have done already? Well, he obviously didn't think she'd already discovered the loss of her key, and that was something she could let him know right away.

"Peaceful?" she echoed. *"Peaceful?* When you've been rifling through my bag – stealing my property – planning to lock me out? Did you really imagine I wouldn't notice? Did you really think I didn't know you were creeping around in my room this morning? I suppose you mean to turn me out when it suits you.

Well, it won't work. I don't intend to be turned out. So if you don't mind, I'll have my key back." She held out her hand.

"Oh, not yet, I think." Thorne sat down and reached for a croissant. "I'm not at all sure it's your key, you see. As far as I'm concerned, it's Jeff's. And until I find out different – well, I think it's better if I take charge of it, don't you?"

"So that you can lock me out," Vary said tightly. "I hope you intend to give me the rest of my property when you do."

"Well, I shan't necessarily lock you out, you see." He smiled at her again, lazily, devastatingly. "As I told you, I prefer to have you under my eye. If what I suspect about you is right, you could have friends in the neighbourhood and I don't much want you getting in touch with them. So, as long as you behave yourself, you're welcome to stay around the cottage. But if you're not a good girl – if you go wandering off for too long – well, I might well decide not to let you back in again when you do come back. So you see—" he finished buttering his croissant and bit off the end "—it's really up to you."

Vary shook her head. "I don't understand. Just what is it you think I'm up to? What friends do you think I've got around here?" She looked at him, her eyes golden in the morning light. "I don't know what you suspect at all," she confessed helplessly. "One minute you seem to think I'm a parasite, just out to spend my father's money, the next, I'm some kind of a spy. Which is it you believe? And what are you hiding that you're afraid I might find out? It's you that has the guilty conscience, Thorne, not me. It's whatever you've got in that locked room that's destroying your trust. If it weren't for that, you'd believe the truth – that I'm just here for a few days' break, that I've got every right to be here."

Thorne pursed his lips, then gave a small shrug. "Maybe you're right. Maybe I am super-sensitive. I just happen to have something to be sensitive about – and if I'm right about you, you'll know what it is." His eyes glinted, blue as the sea behind him. "All right, maybe I'm wrong about you, and it does all seem to be one big confused jumble, but if so, there's no harm done, except maybe to your pride. And we'll leave it at that, shall we? You can stay here until Thursday, in fact, I'd prefer you to. Then I'll contact Jeff and we'll clear the matter up. Meanwhile, if you do take off, don't expect to get back in again. OK?"

Vary reached for a croissant. Thorne was taking all this very coolly, so that's the way she'd play it too. She broke open the steaming, golden roll and began to spread it with cherry jam.

"No, it isn't really OK at all," she said, without glancing up. "But you hold the whip hand, as you've intended to do all along, and there's nothing much I can do against brute force. I just hope that after Thursday, you'll have the grace to apologise. Or get out altogether." She raised her eyes and let them dwell on his face. "Because I mean to telephone Jeff, too, you know. And it may be that I'll be the one to have my suspicions confirmed. Or hadn't you thought of that?"

Vary spent the rest of the day around the cottage. She knew Thorne sufficiently well by now to believe that he meant what he said, and she had no intention of being locked out. In any case, there was no reason at all why she shouldn't do exactly as she'd planned to do here – rest and relax. Accordingly, she dragged Jeff's old garden lounger out onto the grass and stretched herself out on it, wearing a brief yellow bikini that showed up the tan she'd acquired during her travels. When the sun grew too hot, she ran down the sandy beach of the tiny cove and into the cool, rippling waves, then came out again to dry off and revel in the warmth once again.

She didn't see Thorne at all, except when she went into the cottage in the middle of the day to fetch herself some bread and cheese. He had emerged from his room at the same moment and stood in the kitchen, dwarfing it as he always seemed to do to any room. Vary glanced at his broad, massively muscled chest, bare under the unbuttoned blue shirt that set off his own tan, shades deeper than hers, and was immediately, acutely conscious of the skimpiness of her bikini. She caught Thorne's eyes on her body, taking in its slenderness and the small perfection of her breasts, and felt herself flush scarlet. Did he have to look at her like that? She was accustomed enough to having men's glances follow her, but from Thorne, and in this confined space, it seemed different.

"Sorry to disturb you," she said curtly, and bit her lip as she saw the twitch of amusement on his lips, "but I just wanted a piece of bread and a drink of water."

"And what better repast could there be?" he said gravely, but she was sure he was laughing at her. "A jug of wine, a loaf of bread and thou . . . There *is* wine, actually, if you'd like it. And have some of this cheese – it's local and very good – and an apple." He piled the food on to a plate as he spoke and handed it to her with a mock bow.

Vary took it, dismayed to find her hand trembling as their fingers brushed. What was it about this man? He put out an aura of masculinity that seemed almost solid. Scarlet-faced, she muttered a brief and ungracious thank you, and escaped into the garden. She could have done without Thorne following her, but at least there was space out here and she could keep a distance between them.

She couldn't, however, stop him from looking at her and as he sprawled on the grass beside her she was all too aware of his eyes, still moving over her body in that assessing fashion. He'll be able to recognise me anywhere soon, she thought furiously, but there was nothing she could do about it. Determined to ignore him, she turned away and lifted her glass of wine.

"So you've been here quite a few times," Thorne remarked lazily, and she turned her eyes back to him. He had removed his shirt and lay on the grass, propped on one elbow as he ate, clad only in a pair of brief, rather shabby denim shorts. His legs were long, the strength of his thighs evident from the muscles that shaped them, and their tan was as deep as that on his chest and powerful back. He must have spend a long time in the sun to get that colour, Vary thought, and then realised that he was watching her quizzically.

God, she'd been staring at him just as hard as he'd stared at her! Blushing painfully, she looked away, and dragged her mind back to what he'd said.

"Yes – yes, I've been here quite a lot," she stammered. "At least, when Jeff first bought the cottage we all used to come here for holidays, his parents and I. And then I used to come here just with Jeff, if they couldn't manage it. We spent as much time here as we could." Surely he could tell that she was speaking the truth.

"You're pretty fond of Jeff, then."

"Yes, I am. Very fond."

"He's your cousin, you said."

"That's right." Suddenly, she resented this probing. "But he's been more like a brother to me, especially since—" She stopped abruptly; she wasn't going to tell him all about *that*. Thorne watched her for a moment and she was afraid he was going to press the point, but he didn't. He merely went on to ask her if she had seen any of the prehistoric monuments in the area.

"Oh, yes. Jeff's always been interested in them, and I find them fascinating. Especially the standing stones at Carnac – have you been there?" In her enthusiasm, she forgot that she had good reason to distrust this man and turned to face him, drawing her knees up under her and gesticulating with her hands. "The *Alignements*, they're called and they're just outside the town. They stretch for a mile, maybe more – a double row of huge menhirs. Nobody knows what they were for or how they came to be put there. I can stand and stare at them for hours, thinking about the people who did it – the sheer hard labour of erecting them all, the plan that must have been behind it, the reasons." The enormity of it all overwhelmed her, as it always did, and she felt tears sting her eyes. "And there are other monuments all around Carnac, too – the St Michel tumulus that they've excavated and you can go into – but they've spoilt that for me, there's no atmosphere left at all – and the other dolmens that are scattered about." She stopped, remembering suddenly who she was talking to, and flushed again. Thorne was watching her steadily, but there was something else in his eyes now, something Vary didn't wait to analyse before she turned away and drank her wine down with a hurried gulp.

"There's a tumulus on the island in the gulf, just off the village, too," she said, trying to sound careless. "You can get a boat from the jetty."

"Maybe I'll do that." His eyes were still on her as she poured herself some more wine, and he added lazily, "I wouldn't drink too much of that. Not if you're going to lie in this hot sun all afternoon."

Vary's temper rose. "I know just how much I can drink, thank you." She bit into a piece of bread, wishing she hadn't let her feelings carry her away. It was always the same when she was interested in something, her enthusiasm took over and she forgot everything else.

She took a piece of cheese and kept her eyes fixed on the tide, now low and revealing humps of barnacle-covered rocks. Women and children with buckets were beginning to gather, collecting shellfish, and an old man was wandering along the shoreline with a sack.

Thorne shrugged. He finished his lunch, stood up and stretched, looking like some Greek god in the burning sunlight. Or were they fair haired? Vary thought bemusedly, trying to recall the pictures she'd seen in her classics book at school. No, Greeks were dark, with features that simply asked to be sculpted; those sloping planes of cheek and jaw, the aquiline noses, the firmly shaped mouth . . .

"Time to get back to work," Thorne remarked, and picked up his plate and glass. "I thought we'd go out for a meal tonight, the restaurant in the village is quite good. Mostly local foods. They specialise in fish, if you like it."

"I do, and I've been there quite a few times," Vary reminded him.

"Yes, of course. With Jeff." His expression was unfathomable as he gazed down at her.

"With Jeff," she agreed, and turned over to let the sun warm her back.

The afternoon sun, together with the wine she had drunk, soon made Vary feel sleepy. Her head pillowed itself on her arms. Her sleepless night caught up with her and her eyes closed.

It was much later when she woke, and at first she couldn't imagine where she was. Her back was burning, her head felt hot and muzzy and two sizes too large. There was a roaring in her ears, the sound of distant voices that she couldn't place. Someone was speaking to her in tones that sounded furiously angry, insisting that she must do something immediately – but what?

"Oh, God," she moaned, "my head – it's falling apart."

"And I'm not a bit surprised!" She recognised the voice now as Thorne's, and groaned. "Lying out here all these hours in the hot sun – *and* after you've been drinking. Don't you realise how foolish that is? Don't you know the dangers of getting sunburnt? Your back's just about on fire, you're soaked with perspiration and I'll be very surprised if you haven't got a temperature. You'd better get inside straightaway and let me have a look at you."

Vary sat up, still dazed, remembering only when it was too late that she'd unfastened the strap of her bikini top to avoid getting a pale line across her back. The scrap of material dropped away and she saw Thorne's eyes go to her breasts. Hastily, she gathered up the material and held it against her. Thorne reached out and she shrank away from him.

"Oh, for God's sake!" he said impatiently. "D'you think I've never seen a woman before? I'm more concerned about your sunburn right now than your feminine attractions." He gripped her arm, hauling her to her feet, and steadied her as she staggered a little. "You're still half-asleep. Come on – indoors."

Vary let him propel her into the cottage, and sank on

to the settee. She could feel her back scorching now, and knew she would suffer for a day or two until the redness wore off. But it couldn't be too bad; with her dark colouring, she tanned easily and she'd already been protected by frequent sunbathing sessions that summer. It was the dizziness and the headache that were bothering her most, and she knew that Thorne was right when he'd told her she had drunk too much wine.

"I'm all right," she said faintly, as he pressed her head firmly forwards. "Look, you don't need to—"

"You're not all right. You're far too hot and you probably feel sick. And you need some lotion for that back. Have you got anything?"

Numbly, Vary shook her head. He was right, she did feel sick, and she was shaking, but whether that was a symptom of sunstroke or the feel of Thorne's hands on the tender skin of her neck and shoulders, she didn't know.

"I don't use much lotion," she whispered. "Only at first – once I'm brown I don't need it."

"Well, you need it now. And who decreed that you could be immune to skin cancer?" He paused for a moment. "I've got some, I think. Wait here." He disappeared into the small bedroom, returning with a bottle. "It's almost all gone. I'll put it on your back to cool it down while I go to the village and get some more."

Vary sat up straight. "I can do that—" she began, but Thorne had already tipped the white lotion into his palm and begun to apply it. It struck cold, and she gasped

– but the gasp was as much due to Thorne's palm, moving slowly and gently over her skin, as it was to the chill. She closed her eyes, the image of his long fingers imprinted on her brain as clearly as if she could see them, and fought down the sudden longing to turn into his arms. It wasn't a caress, she reminded herself angrily, much as it might feel like one, and she didn't want it to be one, for heaven's sake! What on earth was she thinking of?

All the same, it felt remarkably like a caress as Thorne's long fingers traced gently over the line of her shoulder blades and slid down the length of her spine. Vary was unable to repress a shiver as his hand reached her waist and lay on it momentarily before slipping further down to the line of her bikini pants. For a moment, she thought that he was about to slide them off, but realised almost at once that he was simply smoothing lotion over the line of extra soreness that always seemed to develop where clothing met skin. Or was he? Merely applying lotion didn't have to be this sensual . . . this insinuating . . . did it? Vary lay completely still, knowing that if she moved at all she would be sighing and stretching under his touch, her sunburn and headache forgotten, wanting only to lure his seeking hand further, into more intimate exploration. A deep longing shook her; she wanted desperately to turn into his arms, feel his naked skin against hers, the roughness of hairs against her own smooth, bare breasts; his lips parting hers in a kiss that would start where the other one – so long ago, it seemed – had left off. Her heart thudded, slow and heavy. Her mind whirled. When she closed her eyes, there was nothing in the world but this – this slow, sensuous movement of Thorne's hand on her back, and the turmoil of sensation it aroused in her body.

Thorne's fingertips slid under her arm and touched the side of her breast. There was a moment of complete stillness. Vary could almost hear her own heart beating, and there was a quality in Thorne's silence that made her wonder if he could too. Then, abruptly and with what sounded like a bitten-off, muttered exclamation, he took his hand away and stepped back.

"That's all, I'm afraid." There was an odd harshness in his voice and Vary looked up, her eyes dark and wide, shaken both by her own unexpected reaction and by his sudden withdrawal. What was he thinking? That she'd been trying deliberately to seduce him? Her face burned at the thought. But he had turned, and his face was in shadow. "I'll have to go and get something from the village shop – they've got a reasonable selection there, you don't need anything glamorous. You'd better lie down until I come back."

Deftly, he lifted her feet to the settee and made her lie back. Vary gazed up at him, aware that the yellow top of her bikini was still draped inefficiently over her breasts. She realised that she didn't want him to go; she wanted him to stay here, warm and vital beside her, touching her body as he'd been doing only moments ago . . . Shocked at her own thoughts, she closed her eyes and missed the expression on Thorne's face.

"I'll be as quick as I can," he said raggedly, and she heard him go out, leaving the door open behind him so that a cool breeze drifted in with the hot scent of broom and the salt of the sea.

Vary lay quite still. Her first confusion on waking up, hot from the sun, had disappeared and she knew that she would soon be completely recovered. And now that Thorne's physical presence had been removed, she was slowly returning to her senses and able to try to assess just what had been happening to her.

All right, he was attractive, she'd known that from the first moment she'd seen him, standing there in the doorway of the cottage. She'd been aware of him, physically – yes, and sexually, she had to admit it – ever since they'd met.

That didn't mean she had to let him get to her, did it? It didn't mean she had to give in to her own traitorous body. Because that's all it is, Vary Carmichael, she scolded herself. Sexual attraction – chemistry – nothing more. Something she'd always considered she could handle, since nobody had ever attracted her that powerfully before.

So it's not so easy, she thought grimly. Not so easy to keep your head when a man as magnetic as Thorne is around, both of you half-naked most of the time. But that doesn't mean it can't be done. It doesn't mean he can't be resisted.

In half and hour, maybe less, he'd be back with some more lotion which, this time, she'd apply herself. Meanwhile, she didn't have to be lying here with only a brief pair of bikini pants on when he did return.

Her back was sore, but not unbearable. Slowly, she sat up.

The door in the corner that led to the small bedroom – the door that had been kept locked ever since she arrived – stood open. Thorne had gone in for the lotion and forgotten to lock it again when he came out.

He would be at least half an hour getting to the village and back – perhaps longer if there were other people shopping. Time for her to see inside; time for her to find out just what Thorne was doing here, what secret he was hiding behind that mysterious door.

She might never get another chance like this. Forgetting to fasten her bra, forgetting everything in her surge of excitement, Vary scrambled from the settee and tiptoed towards the door.

Her heart hammered. In a few moments, she would know . . .

Chapter Four

"And just what do you think you're doing in here?"

With a squeak of pure terror, Vary whipped round. Thorne's bulk filled the doorway, his face as ominous as approaching thunder, a threat in every line of his massive body. Cold fear slithered across Vary's skin and she backed away from the fury in his blazing eyes, her hands groping behind her for protection. There was a table there, she knew, that much she'd glimpsed before Thorne had erupted into the room, and she'd seen briefly that it seemed to be set up as some kind of dispensary, with bottles and glass tubes. But before she came into contact with it, Thorne had taken one huge stride towards her and imprisoned her groping hands in his, wrenching them in front of her.

"Don't touch anything there!" The intensity in his voice frightened her more than ever and she gazed up at him, dread darkening her amber eyes to mahogany. Thorne gave her a jerk that brought her hard up against him, transferred both her slender wrists to one hand, and used the other to tip back her head.

"I knew it!" he exclaimed. 'I knew you were spying on me – you've been waiting for an opportunity to get into this room ever since you arrived. And there's no point in trying to deny it now – not now that you've been given that opportunity and taken it so eagerly."

"You – you mean you set me up? You went off, knowing you'd left the door open, knowing I'd go in?"

"Thinking you would," he corrected grimly. "I reckoned that if I'd been wrong about you, you were feeling too grotty to bother. But if you were really keen to find out, you'd get in there no matter how rotten you were feeling. Which is just what you did."

"That proves nothing!" Vary snapped. "I wanted to see inside because this is Jeff's cottage and I wanted to know just what was going on in it. You seem to think I've got some ulterior motive in coming here at all – that I'm a paid spy for someone else, someone who's also interested in what you're doing. Well, I'm not, but I can tell you this – everything you've said and done has made me think that whatever you're up to, it's for nobody's benefit but your own. And looking around now –" Her eyes roamed around the room, taking in thoroughly what she'd assimilated in moments before "—it seems to me that the people most likely to be interested in what you're doing are the police." She glanced over her shoulder at the table, with jars and bottles at one end and the typewriter and piled notes at the other. "What is it you're working on, Mr Thorne?" she demanded, her voice, despite her fear, edged with contempt. "Drugs of some sort? Is that your filthy game? Working out even more evil ways to destroy people, kill and maim them, and all for a fast buck—"

"That's enough!" Thorne's free hand swung back and then slapped her cheek with such force that her head jerked. The crack echoed through the cottage and Vary staggered, her ears ringing. Her cheek felt as if it were on fire, stung by a thousand nettles, and as Thorne released her she put up one hand, hardly daring to touch the burning skin. Tears of pain, humiliation and downright rage filled her eyes.

"You brute! You great, bullying thug! What right do you have to knock me about? Just who do you think you are – taking over my cousin's cottage to use for your vile schemes, keeping me here more or less a prisoner, laying traps for me and then hitting me when I find out just what you're doing?" She stared up at him, eyes spitting fire, anger transcending her fear. "All right, Thorne, do your worst. It can't be any worse than what I'd expect from you. I knew from the first that you weren't to be trusted. No wonder you were afraid of my finding out," she sneered, taunting him even though she knew it must be dangerous. "I only wonder that you didn't dispose of me straightaway, just as no doubt you're wondering too. It would have saved you quite a lot of trouble!"

"You don't know just how near you are to the truth with that statement." His eyes dropped and Vary remembered suddenly that she still wasn't wearing her bikini bra. Her cheeks burnt again, but she tossed her head, determined that mere embarrassment wasn't going to disconcert her now. All the same, the discovery made her feel increasingly vulnerable.

Thorne stood quite still for a moment, his eyes on the curves, less richly-tanned than the rest of her body. Then, with an almost visible effort, he wrenched his head up and said harshly, "You'd better cover yourself up. Here." And he ripped a shirt from the back of a chair and flung it at her.

Startled, Vary caught it and slipped her arms into the sleeves. The garment draped her body like a loose tunic, reaching almost to her knees, and she wrapped it across in front of her, unaware of the frail and defenceless appearance the voluminous folds gave her. Thorne watched her, that odd expression that she'd caught once or twice before, masking his eyes. Then he jerked his head abruptly towards the other room.

"Right. Out of here. I told you before, it's private."

"Private?" Vary glanced again at the bottles and the pile of notes. "I just bet it is! Not the sort of thing you'd want any casual visitor seeing, is it? Or any visitor at all. And you claim to be a friend of Jeff's?" She curled her lip scornfully. "You're not fit to clean his boots for him."

"I daresay you're right," he said coldly, though she could sense the temper simmering beneath his icy tone. "Jeff's a fine man, though I'm not sure just how *you* would know that. And I'm not sure just what you're trying to imply about my activities. You said something about drugs, if I heard right. Maybe you'd like to come out and explain that."

Vary hesitated. She wanted to defy him, to march further into the inner room and examine those bottles and jars more closely, see just what the mountain of typing was all about. But there was a dangerous glint in his eye and his stance, ready as a leopard to spring for the kill, told her that she would get no further than half a step. Shrugging, as if it couldn't matter less, she turned away and followed him.

"I'll get dressed first, if you don't mind," she declared, trying to keep the tremor from her voice. "So if you wouldn't mind waiting outside—"

"Oh, but I would." His voice was silky now. "I'd mind very much indeed. You have the choice – get dressed with me in here, or stay as you are." His own shrug was far more effective than hers had been. "It's up to you."

Vary hesitated, seething, but she knew what her answer must be. There was no way she would dress herself with him in the room, watching. She lifted one shoulder and dropped into the old armchair. It was one she remembered from her childhood, from her aunt's home – Jeff must have brought it over with him at some time. She closed her eyes for a moment, recalling the times when she had sat here, cuddling up to her aunt or uncle, being comforted for her loss. And now they've gone too, she thought desolately, and Grandfather as well. There's no one left now but Jeff and me.

"Are you all right?" Thorne asked suddenly, and her eyelids flew open.

"Yes, of course I am." She summoned up her look of defiance and decided to go into the attack. "Well? Do you deny it?"

"Deny it? Deny what, for God's sake?"

"That you're involved with drugs of some sort." Vary rose to her feet again. "Look, I'm not a fool. I can see you're doing some kind of experiment in there – mixing chemicals. And I know what money there is in drugs these days." Her voice was edged now with real contempt. "Do you know what I think of you and your kind? I think you're despicable. I've seen what happens to those who use drugs. Kids still at school, taking a pill to keep themselves awake at an all-night party. University students who want to keep awake for their studies. Some of them have *died*, you know that? Of course you do! But you don't care, do you? You'll spout some rubbish about how it's more dangerous to cross the road – never mind that if those who died hadn't taken your filthy cocktails they *wouldn't* be dead, that roads and other dangers don't come into it. Never mind that we all do take risks, but we don't have to take your particular sort. Never mind that for every youngster who dies from taking a pill there are a hundred scum like you, still walking the earth, pocketing their money and not giving a damn. Why, if I had my way—"

She stopped. Thorne was watching her with a kind of amazement. If the subject hadn't been so serious, she would have suspected him of laughing at her. But

63

perhaps he was. It wasn't serious for him, was it? Not in the way it was for her.

"All right," she said angrily. "Amuse yourself. But you'll be laughing on the other side of your face when the police see what you're doing here."

He stared at her and she felt a chill of fear as he said, slowly, "Police? Do you really think, Vary, you silly child, that if all you seem to believe about me were true I'd let you get a yard out of this cottage, let alone call the police?"

Vary swallowed. Of course he was right. He was never going to let her give him away. She hadn't a chance of escaping him. All the stories she had heard about drugs and drug pushers ran through her mind. People found dead in mysterious circumstances. People who disappeared without trace. Gangland killings . . . She was acutely aware of how remote the cottage was, how few people knew she was here. *Nobody* knew she was here. Only Jeff had any idea – and by the time he began to wonder why he hadn't heard from her, she could be beyond help.

I shouldn't have let fly like that, she thought, I should have just kept quiet and got away as soon as I could and never come near the place again, at least until it was safe. I should have just kept my mouth shut.

But then she never had been very good at doing that, had she? It had got her into trouble a hundred times. Never as much trouble as this, though.

"Well?" he said. "What shall I do with you? Now that you know so much, I mean. I certainly can't afford to let you go, can I? What do you advise, hmm? Should I keep you prisoner for a while, have my wicked way with you – or should I just get it over with quickly? Which would *you* prefer?"

Terror rose like a sick wave within her. But with it came a kind of last-ditch courage. I won't let him see I'm scared, she thought, lifting her chin. I won't let him see he's won.

"It's rather up to you, isn't it," she retorted, hating the quiver in her voice but keeping the defiance none-theless. "You must be about twice my size and probably three or four times my strength. But whatever you decide – I warn you, I'll fight you every inch of the way."

He raised his eyebrows. "Do you know, I really believe you will." There was a heartbeat of silence. Then he moved forward, so suddenly that Vary leapt back like a startled kitten. He stopped at once, one hand still outstretched, the other running long fingers through his hair.

"Dammit, Vary, don't look like that. I'm not going to hurt you." His face was grim, but for once the anger didn't seem to be directed at her. "My God, what sort of a brute am I, letting a kid like you get so scared? And the way you're standing up to me too – just won't admit you're frightened, will you? Look, relax for a minute, you're as taut as a spring. Sit down again and I'll get you a drink. You look as if you're about to pass out on your feet."

"I'm not . . ." Vary began, but even as she spoke

the room swam before her. She put a hand to her forehead and gave a faint moan, then was only vaguely aware of Thorne's arms about her, of the strength in them as he lowered her to the chair and gently pushed her head forward, between her knees. She felt his palm laid on her back, the splay of his fingers across her shoulder blades. After a few minutes, the singing muzziness began to clear and she lifted her head. He laid her back against the cushions and looked at her.

"You're all in. Stay there."

She heard the tap run in the kitchen and a moment later a glass of cold water was touched gently against her hand. She took it and sipped, feeling the strength return, and glanced at his face.

Her heart shook at the look in his eyes. She opened her mouth, tried to speak but could not utter a word. In that moment, he lowered his lids, and when their eyes met again his were shuttered, veiled. I imagined it, she thought. Or maybe it's a kind of hypnotism. I mustn't start trusting him now.

"Let's start again, shall we?" he said quietly. "I've got a feeling we've got our wires crossed somewhere along the line."

"Oh yes?" she answered coolly. "Well, perhaps you'd like to explain just where. Because all I've done is tell you the truth. I'm not sure the same can be said about you."

Thorne sighed and ran his fingers through his hair again. "I've told you no lies—"

"You've told me nothing at all. Except that you definitely have something to hide." This is madness, she thought, I still can't stop goading him. I ought just to keep quiet. But some little demon inside urged her to continue. "You as good as told me that the first minute we met. Accusing me of spying on you – of giving information about you to my friends, whoever they might be." She challenged him with her look. "So what kind of information do you think I might be after, Mr Thorne Whoever-You-Are? Just let me ask you once again, what *do* you have in that room, in all those little bottles?"

"You never let up, do you?" he marvelled. "You could be in danger of your life and still you won't give way. You know, I really do admire you—"

"And you can cut the sarcasm!" she broke in, all the more furiously because she knew he was right. She might still be in mortal danger, even though he had given her water instead of knocking her on the head. And it wasn't going to help her at all that she might be right – it could only make things worse.

But as she'd told him, she wasn't going to go out without a fight.

Thorne gave her that strange, heart-stopping glance again.

"I meant it," he said quietly. "I really do admire you. You've got a lot of courage. And I believe you really do feel strongly about drugs—"

"Well, of course I do. Everyone with any decency does. But you wouldn't know about that, would you?"

she added with scathing bitterness. "You're in the business, after all."

He whistled softly, and shook his head. "Thank your lucky stars you're wrong about that, Vary. I can't imagine any drugs dealer letting you live, after you'd spoken to him like that. But fortunately for you, I'm not a drugs dealer, nor do I have anything at all to do with drugs – not in the way you mean."

"So you don't deny you are doing experiments in there?" Vary's eyes went to the door to the inner room, securely locked once again. "You don't deny they're to do with drugs?"

"No, but—"

"So just what are you doing?" Her heart quickened with fear again, but she held his glance. *"Tell* me."

He stared at her for a full minute, then shook his head again. "I can't. I daren't trust you. I wish I could, but—"

"But you still don't believe me." Her shoulders drooped. It seemed vitally important now, somehow, that Thorne should believe her, that he should trust her. "I swear I've told you the truth."

"Yes. I believe you have." Her heart lifted." But I still can't tell you, Vary. You see – I've lost faith in my own judgement. I've wanted to trust you all along, but the facts seemed to tell against you. And when I came in and found you in that room – well, it seemed that everything I didn't want to believe was true after all. But then you went for me about what you thought I was doing, and that turned all my ideas on their heads

68

again. And now – I just don't know what to believe."
He sighed and pushed his fingers through his hair once
more. "I can't make up my mind – and I'm not used to
that feeling. I don't like it. But while I'm feeling this
way, all I can do is ask for proof."

"Jeff," she said. "Jeff will tell you."

"Jeff," he said, and nodded. "Of course. And he'll
tell *you* about *me*."

There was a short silence. Vary sipped again at her
water. She still felt shaky, as if she had been through
some traumatic experience. And so I have, she thought.
I really believed he was going to do something dreadful
to me. And even now, I don't know. He could still
be stringing me along, lying, winning me over in that
strange, hypnotic way . . . If only I could talk to Jeff
now, if only he could tell me it's all right . . .

Thorne rose abruptly to his feet.

"We'll go phone again," he said, and Vary jumped
as if he'd been reading her mind. "We both need
reassurance and Jeff's the only one that can give it.
That's if—" he glanced at her "—we're both telling
the truth."

"Well, I certainly am," she said with a return to
her former heat, and he grinned, almost unwillingly.

"Either you're a very good actress, or you really are
telling the truth." He gave her a more concerned look.
"Are you sure you're fit to go out?"

"Well, I'm not letting you go on your own," she
retorted. "And I don't propose to let you lock me

in here either." She stood up cautiously and to her relief the room stayed steady about her. "I'm all right now."

They went out of the cottage together and Thorne locked the door. Vary sighed a little. Jeff had never bothered to lock it in the old days, not if he was only going to the village. This spot was so hidden, so tucked away, it had never seemed necessary. But now that Thorne was here, it all seemed different. He really did have something to hide, something that was clearly important to him, and if it wasn't drugs, what could it be?

With a sudden return to her fear, Vary realised that he hadn't actually denied he was working on drugs of some sort. Not in the way you mean, he'd said, but what other way was there?

No, there were still questions that needed to be answered. And as they walked together along the lane, between hedges of brambles and roses, Vary wondered if even Jeff was going to be able to supply the answers. And what would happen if he couldn't . . .

As they approached the telephone box, Thorne gave an exclamation of annoyance.

"Damn! I haven't got any change. And I've used my last telephone card."

"It doesn't matter." Vary's suspicions returned at once. "I've got my charge-card with me. It was one of the things Jeff insisted I take on my trip, so that I'd never be unable to phone if I needed help."

"He looks after you, that cousin of yours," Thorne commented, an odd note in his voice.

"He does," Vary agreed equably, feeling in control for once. "We're very close, Jeff and I. As you will see." She fished the card from her purse and they entered the telephone box.

Immediately, she was conscious, as she'd known she would be, of Thorne's closeness. The kiosk was tiny, even smaller than British ones, it seemed, and the air inside was stale and warm. Vary could smell the aftershave he used and, beneath that, an earthier scent – a scent that was composed of many things: soap, sweat, warm, sweet breath and something else she couldn't identify, barely knew she could smell – a scent that spoke to her senses and brought out her nerve-ends in a tingle of spiralling excitement and desire.

Stop it, she told herself frantically, *stop* it. And she pushed her charge-card into the slot, with shaking hands.

"Shall I dial?" Thorne's voice sounded husky. Vary shook her head and lifted the telephone.

"I'll do it. I know the number as well as I know my own." She pushed the buttons swiftly, hearing the tiny beeps of acknowledgement, then held the receiver to her ear, waiting for the connection. "It's ringing now." Be there, Jeff, she begged silently, be there.

The ringing tone sounded too close to be all those miles away across the Channel, and even at this tense moment Vary marvelled, as she always did, at the wonder of a world-wide network that enabled someone in one country to contact and talk direct to someone hundreds, thousands of miles away in another. Even in another hemisphere. People just took it for granted. And now that the Internet . . . she became aware of Thorne shifting impatiently beside her, and was reminded sharply of his presence, close and warm beside her.

"No answer?" She caught his ironic gaze on her and her patience snapped.

"Try for yourself." She thrust the receiver at him. "Dial the number – make sure I'm not trying to deceive you."

He shrugged and did as she bade. But once again there was nothing but the ringing tone, far away in England.

"Seems he's not in. Pity he doesn't have an answering machine." Thorne replaced the receiver. "Not that it would help much in this case, since he can't return the call."

"We'll just have to keep trying." Vary was glad to escape from the confined little box. She frowned. "I wonder where he is. I'd have expected him to be back at home by now."

"Probably popped out for some milk." Thorne glanced at her. "Though in a way it doesn't really matter, does it."

"What do you mean?"

"We both dialled the same number. Which proves we both know Jeff, and know his number well enough not to have to look it up." He nodded at her and held out his hand. "I think that vindicates us both, don't you?"

Vary stared at him. She looked at the hand he held out and moved to take it – then snatched her own back again.

"Does it? I don't think so. It proves *I* was telling the truth – but it doesn't prove anything about you. You could simply have watched me dial and then memorised the number. It doesn't mean you already knew it."

"But I did offer to dial first," he pointed out. "Then you'd have seen at once whether I knew it or not. Besides, if I *didn't* know the number, why would I now believe that you did? You could have been dialling anything."

"And risked some stranger answering?" But Vary's head was beginning to whirl with all these complications. "I don't think it proves anything."

Thorne was laughing, and she stared at him in astonishment. It was her first glimpse of the man he could be as his face suddenly lightened, his eyes dancing. She felt a sudden warmth, as if something inside her had begun to melt, but the feeling was followed swiftly by an irritation that was almost a defence.

"I don't see anything to laugh at!"

"Oh, Vary, you must! It's just too silly for words. *Obviously* we're both on the level. We've got to be. Look—" he held out his hand again "—why don't we agree to talk it through and have done with all this suspicion. I believe you – right? I'm convinced you wouldn't have gone through this charade if you hadn't been straight, and I do know you dialled Jeff's number. And even without that as proof, your outburst against drugs earlier would have more than three-quarters convinced me." He gave her a thoughtful look. "One day you must tell me just why you feel so strongly."

"I'll tell you that now. One of Jeff's pupils almost died from taking Ecstasy a couple of years ago. A bright, intelligent girl who tried it just once, and almost lost her life. There've been other youngsters who weren't so lucky. And even before that—" She shuddered. "I just hate the whole scene."

"I see." His voice was sombre. "Yes, I can understand your feelings. And it might help you to know that I feel just the same. Drugs, alcohol, all the hype that goes with them, they're responsible for a lot of damage. But—"

"So why are you working with them?" she burst out. "What are you doing in the cottage?"

"It's not like that. I've told you—"

"Then what is it like?" She stopped and faced him. "If it's all so innocent, why all the secrecy? Tell me." She stared at him imploringly. "*Trust* me, Thorne."

"Yes," he said quietly, and took her hand in his. He held it, looking down at her palm, and then covered it with his other hand. "That's just what I mean to do."

Chapter Five

They began the walk back to the cottage in silence. Vary glanced sideways at Thorne once or twice, but his face was inscrutable and she could not tell what he was thinking. Somehow, thought, it looked softer, the harsh lines smoothed out, and she no longer had the sensation that she was walking into danger.

Or did she? There was still danger there, she knew – danger for her, personally, with this man who was so contradictory, so implacably, coldly angry one moment, and alight with laughter the next. She thought again of that moment of laughter and the glimpse it had given her of a different Thorne, and she remembered her first impression of him – a man so devastatingly attractive that she would have crossed busy roads to be near him, crossed oceans, crossed the world . . .

Vary brought her thoughts up short, with a swift gasp and a hand to her throat. Was that why she'd stayed in the cottage? Was it because she couldn't bear to leave? Did it, perhaps, have nothing to do with Jeff at all?

Thorne caught her gasp and stopped at once, glancing

at her in concern. "Are you all right? Do you want to stop and rest?"

"No. No, I'm fine." But her voice shook and he touched her arm as if afraid she might fall. His touch was like fire, a thin, burning sensation that ran up her arm and directly into her heart, making it kick and tremble in her breast.

Vary stared down at his fingers. What was happening to her?

"Sit here in the shade for a few minutes." He drew her down on to the grassy bank at the side of the lane, under the shade of a spreading hawthorn tree. "You're all in. Is it the heat? Does it normally affect you like this?"

"No," she said and lifted her eyes to his. "No, it never does. I . . . ." She faltered and her words died away. For a few moments – or was it eternity? – the whole world seemed still.

Thorne's eyes were suddenly dark, their sapphire blue reduced to a thin, burning rim around the widened black pupils. Vary sensed the minute changes in the muscles around them, in the tension quivering in the heavy lids, in the tiny flicker somewhere deep within his cheeks. As if mesmerised, she stared into their strange depths; and as if mesmerised, he gazed unblinkingly back.

"Vary?"

His voice was low, husky, more a tremor in the air than a sound. Its vibrations touched her heart, which trembled again in response. Vary felt her bones melt and she put a shaking hand to her forehead.

What was happening to her?

She had asked the question twice now, and deep within something stirred. An answer, perhaps – but was it an answer she wanted to hear? She shook her head abruptly, so that the world sang and spun around her, and she curled her body away from him, away from his electrifying touch.

"What is it?" Again, that husky voice, as if he, too, were asking what was happening, to him as well as to her, to them both, as if he too were feeling the mystery of the moment. I can't handle this, Vary thought frantically. It was better when we were enemies. I can't cope.

"Vary?"

"No," she said, finding her voice at last. "No, Thorne. It's all right. I'm all right. Maybe it is the heat. It's never affected me before, I'm a lizard usually, but there's always a first time, isn't there?" She was babbling, she knew it, she must sound a real airhead, but she couldn't help that. Anything to stop him looking at her like that, anything to stop him speaking in that husky voice, anything to stop the wild sensations beating at her mind. "Let's get back. I probably need a long, cool drink. Dehydration, you know—" And she was on her feet, still shaky but determined to stay clear of him, determined that he shouldn't touch her again, determined above all not to look into those burning blue eyes.

It was no more than five minutes before they were back in the cool, dim house. Thorne bade her sit down again in the armchair while he fetched her a drink, and

Vary was glad by now to let him do it. As before, she laid her head against the back of the chair and once again he touched her wrist with the side of the glass. She took it, avoiding the touch of his fingers, and sipped gratefully.

"Thanks. That's what I needed."

He didn't look at her as he stood sipping his own drink. It was as if he were as keen to avoid her glance and touch as she was to avoid his, she thought, and immediately brushed aside the unexpected stab of pain that this thought brought with it. For a few moments neither of them spoke. When Thorne broke the silence, the huskiness had gone and his voice was strong again.

"Do you feel able to talk?"

"Of course." His abrupt tone strengthened her and she felt a welcome return of her old defiance. She lifted her head and met his gaze with some of the same challenge. "How about you? Are you willing to tell me just what you're doing here?"

"You seem to have made up your mind about that already." Thorne dragged a chair towards him and sat astride it, leaning his arms along the back and still keeping himself between Vary and the door. "I'm a drug-runner, that's the idea, isn't it? Cooking up new and worse concoctions to drive people crazy while milking them of every penny they've got." His face was sombre as he gazed at her. "I certainly don't seem to have made a brilliant first impression on you, do I?"

Vary dropped her glance, feeling unaccountably

gauche. She had to admit, Thorne didn't look like a drug-runner – not like her idea of one, anyway. He didn't talk or behave like one, either. And although he had struck her – and struck her hard – she had a feeling that it was only because he'd been provoked beyond endurance.

But why? Because she'd hit on the truth? Or because she couldn't have been farther away from it?

"Tell me about yourself, Vary," Thorne said, and his voice was unexpectedly gentle. So gentle that tears stung her eyes again and she had to bite her lips and clench her hands to prevent them from falling.

"Look—" Thorne leaned across to her and covered her small fists with his hands – big, warm hands with long fingers which she'd always thought were a sign of a sensitive nature. She stared at them, wondering why she hadn't noticed them in the first place. Had she been wrong about him all along the line? "Look, Vary, we can't go on like this, fighting all the time, pulling in opposite directions. Why don't we put our cards on the table? You've been making a lot of mistakes about me, and maybe you were justified in that. And maybe I've been making mistakes about you, too. But we'll only know if we're completely open and honest with each other."

"But I have been—" Vary began, and he shook his head.

"Not entirely. There are things I don't know about you, Vary. Things like just why you're taking this trip – it's a long one and has to be expensive. Why are you doing it on your own, and how can you afford it? You don't really strike me as a spoilt daddy's darling. And if you were, you wouldn't be staying in cheap inns – yes, I'm afraid I had quite a good look through your bag this morning. You've been making your money last, presumably so that you could see as much as possible. Daddy's girl would have settled for somewhere glamorous to blow the lot." He tilted his head to one side. "So why? What's it all about?"

Vary took a deep breath. "All right. I'm not a daddy's girl." Her voice quivered. "As a matter of fact, I don't have a father at all – or a mother. Both my parents were killed in an air crash when I was fifteen. I was their only child so I inherited what they left, not much, just the house and some savings, but it was more than most fifteen-year-olds have in the bank. But I'm not spending that. It was kept in trust for me and invested, and so far I haven't touched a penny."

"So what happened to you?" Something in his voice told her he was believing her at last. "I guess Jeff's parents took you in, is that right?"

"No. I lived with my grandfather. His home was near ours and Uncle Mike and Aunt Nancy lived fifty miles away. They would have taken me, but between us all it was agreed that I'd be better off staying where I'd always lived, with my own friends and the same school and everything." Her eyes misted at the memories. "But they were very good to me – took me on holidays, had me for weekends and so on. And Jeff was marvellous."

"Mm . . . Jeff." Thorne paused. "You told me how fond of him you are."

"Yes, I am," Vary said frankly. "I don't honestly know if I could have got through without him."

There was a short silence. Thorne broke it by saying, "And this trip?"

"Grandfather died," Vary said in a low voice. "I stayed with him after I left school, he was getting old and he only had me really, Uncle Mike and Aunt Nancy were on my father's side of the family. I went to college near home and took a course in hotel reception and management, and I was able to get a job locally too. By then, he was needing me as much as I'd needed him because he was crippled with arthritis and hardly able to walk in the end. But he'd always been a keen traveller and he knew I wanted to travel too. He used to urge me to go, but I couldn't leave him. He left me all his money – again, just his house and the bit he'd saved – with instructions to use it for seeing as much of the world as I could. So as the job I was in folded soon afterwards, I decided to see Europe. And it seemed only right to make the money last as long as possible."

"And improving your languages, I think you said. Any particular reason for that?"

Vay blinked. She had almost forgotten that first conversation, when she'd tried to persuade him that she had a right to be here, and given up. Evidently Thorne hadn't. "Yes, that's right. I – I just happen to like learning languages. I've got a flair for it, I suppose, and I thought it might be useful one day."

"Useful to whom?"

"Well – to me or to – to someone else, I suppose." Vary floundered, not understanding the drift of his questions. She shrugged helplessly. "It can't do any harm, can it?"

"Certainly it can't." Thorne's dark eyes were thoughtful. "And would you like to be useful to others?"

"Yes, I think I would," Vary said slowly. "Being a hotel receptionist isn't bad – you're giving a service. But I sometimes felt there ought to be more to it than pampering people in hotel rooms, booking theatre tickets for them and ringing for taxis. Life's comfortable enough for them already."

Thorne said nothing for a few minutes. Then he glanced up and met her eyes, and she was surprised and oddly cheered to find that the hostility had gone from his face. For the first time, he was looking at her as if she were a reasonable human being, with a right to her place on earth, and she felt immeasurably warmed.

"All right," he said. "I believe you – though I'll still have to check with Jeff. You'll see why in a minute." He paused. "You've been straight with me, Vary," he said quietly. "Now I'll be straight with you."

Vary watched him. He was looking past her now, his eyes fixed on the wall behind her but not as if he were seeing it, more as if his eyes were filled with pictures of another life, another world. She let her own eyes dwell on his face, examining it for the first time without feelings of hostility, suspicion or fear. She found to her surprise that it wasn't simply an attractive face, conventionally good-looking with the frame of black hair, the smoothly-planed line of brow and jaw, the firm lips, there was character there too, and strength. The deep-blue eyes were thoughtful, the mouth sensitive, and there were tiny lines in the tanned skin that could only come from laughter.

"I told you my name was Thorne," he said at last, "because I didn't want you to know my full name. I wasn't sure about you – I thought you might be a spy, in which case you'd know it anyway. But I half-believed that you *didn't* know, and I was afraid that if you found out who I was, the privacy I so badly needed would be destroyed. You might have got all excited and started telling other people or, worse still, you might have decided that here was a good chance for a bit of notoriety, and rung up one of the English newspapers."

Vary stared at him. "But why? Who *are* you?" She frowned. The way he spoke, it sounded as if he must be royalty at least, and yet – she shook her head. "Look, I'm sorry, but your fame just hasn't reached me. Perhaps I've been too busy with Grandad's illness and death, and then coming abroad. I don't know anyone called Thorne – unless that's not your real name at all?"

"Oh yes, it's my real name." He grinned ruefully. "Well, that'll teach me to be conceited! Evidently I'm not so well known as I thought." He paused. "The name Thorne Moran means nothing to you?"

"Thorne Moran," Vary repeated slowly. Then memory

began to filter back. "Thorne *Moran*? But of course! You're the historical writer – they're televising your saga about the Indian Mutiny – yes, of *course* I've heard of you. Everyone in England's talking about the series, and nobody knows where you are – the papers are going mad. And all the time, you've been here in Jeff's cottage!"

"That's right," he said quietly, his eyes fixed on hers, and Vary realised suddenly what he was doing by telling her this. He was trusting her. Trusting her not to give him away, to tell the first newspaper she could contact. Trusting her to keep a secret that was evidently important to him.

Was he going to trust her with more?

"I shan't tell anyone," she assured him. "But why are you here? The writing I can understand—" her glance went to the closed door as she thought of the table with its strange load "—but what's all the rest of it about? The jars and bottles full of powders and liquids. What are they for?"

"To know that, you have to know something else about me." Thorne paused, his eyes still on her face. "I've never gone in for publicity. I enjoy writing my historical novels, but they're almost a relaxation – a hobby – and an expression of things I think people ought to know, or at least to be able to know. But I've always kept a low profile where the novels are concerned, because I didn't want them to interfere with what I consider to be my real work."

"Your real work?" Fascinated, Vary leaned forward,

pushing up the loose sleeves of the shirt. "But what *is* your real work?"

"I'm a doctor," he said quietly. "I've been working in India for the last eight years, first as a practitioner, and then in research. I've been researching new cures for some of the horrific diseases that attack the under-nourished people of some of the most poverty-stricken areas there. It's taken a long time. The research wasn't begun by me and I'm not the only one working on it, but at last we've begun to get somewhere. We've reached the stage where reports have to be written and published. As soon as that's done, we can go on to find a producer of the new drug – it's almost as good as aspirin or penicillin for some of the diseases that have never had a cure before – and then we can really begin to achieve results." His face was alight, his eyes blue fire as he talked. "That's what I've been doing here: getting all the paperwork done. The jars and bottles contain the ingredients for the new drug. Oh, I couldn't do any experiments here, as such, you need conditions of absolute hygiene for that kind of work. But somehow it helps me to have them there in front of me – call them a kind of talisman, if you like. It's meant a hell of a lot of writing and typing. That's what's been holding me up – the typing. I'm strictly a two-finger man! But I didn't dare get anyone in to help."

"But why not?" Vary brushed back a tendril of soft, dark hair, and then realised. "Oh, because you were afraid of spies. But *why*?"

"Life is harsh out in the world of big business,"

Thorne said grimly. "Even among the companies that produce drugs to cure people and save their lives. They're all in it to make money, after all. And some are less scrupulous than others."

"You mean—?"

"There are one or two of the shadier companies who would dearly like to acquire the formula for this new drug, and they wouldn't be too choosy about how they came by it. There's a lot of money to be made. *We*, my colleagues and I, want to get it out on the open market, where it can be produced as cheaply as possible for the widest possible use. Others might not be so disinterested."

"I see. But surely the people you work with – they must have secretaries."

"We work on a shoestring. All the money possible goes into the health clinics we've set up out there. Obviously, it's a waste of my abilities in a way for me to do work like copy-typing, but I was due for some leave and I decided to spend it this way. And even if I had a typist, we'd have to work so closely together that it wouldn't be any saving of my time." He brought his eyes back to Vary's face, a smooth golden oval in its frame of snuff-brown hair. "So there you have it. The mystery's solved – not nearly so interesting a mystery as you'd expected, I'm afraid."

"Much *more* interesting," Vary retorted. Her mind was busy with a whole new set of pictures: Thorne in white coat, bending over wide-eyed Indian children, talking to them gently as his eyes and fingers probed and his mind made yet another sickening diagnosis; Thorne in the laboratory, studying glass phials that bubbled with coloured liquids, gazing down through a microscope at cultures that would help to bring about a breakthrough. Her blood stirred. While she had been sitting behind a hotel desk booking theatre tickets for well-fed businessmen, he had been devoting his life to the sick and starving. "You're a really useful person," she said slowly. "You make me feel just what you called me once – a parasite."

"Oh, you don't have to think like that," he said quickly. "I was overreacting; I've been sensitive about it since I left India, I know that. Everyone can't go out there and help. People have to get on with living their own way of life – there has to be a standard of civilisation, we can't all degenerate into mud huts and tribal customs just because half the world can't struggle out of them. And the civilisation you've enjoyed gives us the facilities we need. We couldn't cope without it."

"No, I suppose not." Her lips twisted wryly. "All the same, I can understand your reaction to that *Boeuf à la Bourguignonne*. It must have seemed almost obscene."

"Well, I must admit it did, after years of watching people subsist on a bowl of rice a day – if they were lucky. But I was overreacting there, too, obviously it doesn't help them if we starve or deprive ourselves, not unless we give the money we save to one of the charities or medical missions. Which is what I do, incidentally. I do live fairly sparingly so I can do that, while I'm away. All the same, I enjoy a good meal as much as the next man, as long as it's made from local foods, foods which someone's producing for a living, and not exotic and elaborate ingredients that are imported at inflated prices simply to satisfy an ego."

"Like fresh strawberries in January," Vary suggested, and he nodded.

"And the first grouse of the season, rushed down to London to be served to specially favoured clientele."

"Caviare from the Baltic," Vary added, and he gave her a sudden smile, a smile so warm that it took her breath away. At the same moment, his own eyes widened; and they sat quite still, glances locked, as the moment stretched like thin elastic, dangerously taut, tense with hidden undercurrents.

Vary dragged her eyes away at last and gave what she knew was an unnaturally high-pitched laugh. "This shirt's enormous on me! I'd better go and find something else to put on."

"It looks fine to me," Thorne said, and she gave him a quick, almost frightened look. His eyes were dark with an emotion her senses shied away from. She was almost sorry that they'd cleared the air and dismissed their mutual hostility; at least when he'd suspected her of spying and she'd suspected him of God knew what, she'd known where she stood. Now – well, what *was* going to happen now? They had accepted each other as having an equal right to be in the cottage. So, did she continue to spend her time here, while he went on with his work? Or what?

"Look," she said hastily, still trying to find a way

to take that disturbing intensity from his gaze, "why don't you let me help you with that typing? You know now that I'm not a spy. I want a break from travelling but I'd much rather spend it in doing something useful than just lazing around on the beach. And if it'd get your work done quicker, if it'd be any help – well, I'd be pleased to . . ." Her voice faded as she realised that her words had if anything deepened the expression in his eyes. But it was too late now. She'd offered, and she couldn't back out. And, anyway, she discovered with some surprise, she didn't *want* to back out. The idea of helping Thorne with his report was exciting. She had almost been there with him as he'd described the conditions in India; she'd been horrified, pitying, and she'd found herself burning with the desire to *do* something. This could be it.

"You'd actually do that?" Thorne asked. "You'd spend your days indoors typing? I warn you, some of it's not pretty reading and the rest is almost incomprehensible. It wouldn't be easy."

"That doesn't matter, as long as you're around to make sure I don't make any stupid mistakes, check up on medical terms and so on."

"Oh, I'll be around," Thorne said slowly. "But why should you do it? You're on holiday, this is supposed to be a rest."

"I'd also like to do something useful," she reminded him. "So, how about it? After all, if we finish it early, *you* could have a rest too. And I'm sure you need one.

From what you've been saying, you haven't had a break in years."

"No, I haven't. This was supposed to be it – and it is, a complete break, even if I do have to work. But it would certainly be pleasant to have a few days free of all commitments, knowing everything's neatly tied up . . ." He thought for a few minutes, long fingers rubbing his chin, then turned to her. "All right, you're on. You can be my unpaid, overworked, exploited typist – on one condition." His eyes were dancing and Vary felt her heart give a tiny kick.

"And that is?"

"That you spend whatever time I've got left, with me, showing me the sights. Helping me to have the first real holiday I'll have had for years. I couldn't do it without you," he added solemnly. "I've forgotten how. And I have a feeling that we could both benefit by getting to know each other better – so what do you say?"

Vary met his eyes. You're being a fool, a voice told her. You were right to begin with, this man's not only attractive, he's dangerous. Get involved with him, and you'll be risking a change in your entire life, and it might be a change you can't cope with.

She knew she would be wise to refuse his suggestion, to back out of her own impulsive offer. If she left the cottage now and went on her way, there would be no harm done. Nothing to show for their encounter but a few memories and a picture of a lean, dark face, a pair of sapphire eyes and thick black hair. An occasional wistfulness.

If she stayed . . .

"Yes, all right," she said, and her mouth smiled back at him of its own accord. "I'll stay as long as you want me to."

Chapter Six

"**W**ow! It's *freezing!*"

Vary collapsed into the waves, gasping with shock. The water, so early in the morning, before the sun had had time to warm it, was icy. And the spray of droplets showered over her by Thorne as he crashed ahead of her before flinging himself into a fast crawl, didn't help at all. But she knew that, once wet, she would soon become accustomed to the temperature, and she took a deep breath and plunged after him.

Thorne had set off as if determined to swim the Atlantic but when he turned his head and saw Vary following him, her dark hair streaming behind her like the tail of a waterborne comet, he rolled onto his back and waited. His eyes glowed as she came level, and he shook the water from black hair that gleamed like polished jet. His grin was wide and infectious and Vary smiled back, wondering how she could ever have thought him harsh.

"Marvellous, isn't it?" he said, and stretched his body easily along the smooth surface of the water. Vary watched enviously; she had never acquired the knack of floating like that, always having to keep hands and feet moving slightly to avoid going under. But Thorne's big body looked as relaxed as if he were in bed. She could almost imagine him turning to her, reaching for her, drawing her into his arms and keeping her afloat too as they kissed . . .

It wasn't in the least likely to happen, though. Since their long talk, far into the night, when they'd learned at last to trust each other, their relationship had changed dramatically, and not, Vary sometimes caught herself thinking, in the way she wanted. There had been no more smoothing on of sunburn lotion, no more kisses. It was as if Thorne had forgotten she was a woman at all. As if he'd decided to treat her as another man.

When she'd agreed to stay in the cottage and help him with his work, Vary had told herself she was being a fool, because Thorne spelt danger. Now, it seemed, she'd been wrong, he was treating her with scrupulous correctness. So why wasn't she pleased about it?

"Feel like a swim across the bay?" Thorne enquired, and she glanced at the distance he'd indicated and shook her head.

"I'm a potterer, not a long-distance racer," she declared. "You can go, I'll head back to the beach. I'm getting a bit cold, anyway."

Thorne nodded and turned over to settle into his fast crawl again, while Vary trod water and watched. His body looked as if it had been made to cut through water like a fast powerboat, big, yet streamlined, muscles coming into play like the well-oiled components of a precision machine, limbs moving effortlessly to thrust aside the water and send him streaking along its surface. Within minutes the black head was all that could be seen in the swell, looking like a seal as it drove purposefully through the rolling waves. Only Vary's imagination could show her the powerful length of the body, the rich glow of the tanned skin over sinuous muscles, the dynamic propulsion of iron-hard calves and thighs moving as rhythmically as pistons to send him forwards through the foam.

With a sudden twist of her own body, she turned and made for the shore, irritably aware of her own weak performance in comparison with Thorne's. What was wrong with her anyway? she thought crossly as she emerged from the water and began to towel her body rather more vigorously than was necessary. She didn't want Thorne to make advances to her, did she? She was only too well aware of her own reactions, of the way her own body would betray her if it got the chance, and she hadn't wanted that to happen. So why did she keep thinking of him like this? Why was he like a magnet to her, drawing her close only to repel her when she got too close? Why couldn't she resist him, forget him, treat him as she'd treated every other man to come into her life so far?

The truth was something she didn't want to face, but as she stood there on the beach, watching Thorne plough easily through the water with the early morning sun glinting off his shining head, she forced herself to square up to it. You're no better than anyone else,

Vary Carmichael, she told herself ruthlessly. You fancy
Thorne Moran like crazy, and you'd like nothing better
than to go to bed with him, and that's all there is to it.
All you've got to do is decide whether to stick to your
principles, or give in.

That's if he wants to as well, she reminded herself
caustically. It might just be that he doesn't – that he
treats you casually because that's just the way he feels.
That he doesn't even *see* you as a woman.

The thought was oddly depressing.

The early-morning swim had become part of their
routine, and it refreshed them both. It had also become a
ritual for whichever of them was ready first – and it was
usually Vary, because once Thorne got into the water he
seemed increasingly reluctant to come out – to walk into
the village for the fresh croissants that they both agreed
were an essential way of starting the day. They tended
to linger over these and the coffee that Thorne would
have ready when she returned, sitting in the garden to
let the sun warm their hair dry and wallowing, there was
no other word for it he'd remarked lazily one morning,
in the scent of the dew steaming from the grass and the
gold and blush-pink flowers of the broom.

That was the best moment of the day for Vary;
a blissful hiatus when the world was still and there
might have been no other human for a thousand miles
or more. She would have given a great deal for it to
go on, stretching idyllically through the day until the
sun turned the sky to a blaze of saffron and coral and

the shadows of evening touched their faces, and night brought the gleam of starlight to the veiled mystery of Thorne's fathomless eyes.

But it never did go on. Thorne would sigh, stretch out his long legs and push the hair back from his forehead with long, restless fingers, and she would know exactly what he was going to say. "Time for work," he'd remark, as if it were a new idea, and she would reflect ironically that if they were married she'd probably get to screaming point at this predictability. Not that he was predictable in any other way and not that she was ever likely to find out, since they'd never come anywhere near being married . . . She thrust back her own sigh, and got up to take the coffee jug, plates and mugs back to the kitchen. Simply because it was more efficient that way, she usually washed up, did any tidying that was necessary and made her own bed while Thorne looked over their work of the previous day and planned today's. Then she joined him in the small workroom, where the door now stood open all day long, and they forgot about the sunshine outside and concentrated on what had to be done.

She was in an unusually thoughtful mood this morning as she shook out her sheets and spread them smoothly back over the big bed. It was a strange relationship, this one that was evolving with Thorne Moran. Their sleeping arrangements, for instance, they'd changed on that first night after Thorne had caught her investigating his work. Once he'd decided to trust her, it seemed, all his instincts had about-turned. Where before he'd made no bones about leaving her to curl up on the settee, he now insisted that she have the bed. And where she had once been furious that he didn't do just that, she'd been reluctant to accept, pointing out that he was so much bigger, he needed the extra room, emphasising that she was perfectly comfortable on the settee. His cool reply that he was quite happy to use the small bed in the workroom had left her without an answer, and she'd been forced to give in. And that was how it had been all along the line – Thorne stating the terms and Vary accepting them. And so far, she'd been quite happy to do so. But how long it would continue, she didn't know. Vary was accustomed to stating her own terms from time to time, and she had a suspicion that if she did so with Thorne – *when* she did so with Thorne – there might be fireworks.

Well, there was no sense in worrying about that. Since their long talk, they had got on better than she'd ever dared imagine. Except for this problem of his not wanting to treat her as a woman, and her increasing desire that he should.

Then there was the problem of Jeff. Vary paused in her bedmaking, her brow creased with worry. Although they'd continued to try to telephone him, ringing his number several times a day, they'd still had no reply.

"What about his neighbours or friends?" Thorne had suggested as they had wandered back from the telephone box the previous afternoon. "Do you know anyone who might have any information?"

"I don't." Vary felt helpless and frustrated. "I mean,

I know some of his friends of course, but only by their Christian names and I don't know where they live. And since Jeff moved I don't know any of his neighbours. He sold his parents' house after my uncle died." She swallowed the lump that still rose to her throat at the thought of her aunt and uncle, both gone. It seemed so unfair that both she and Jeff should lose their parents so young. "It seems impossible to contact anyone."

"Well, I don't suppose there's anything to worry about really," Thorne said after a pause. "I daresay he's just taken off for a few days' holiday somewhere. He might even be on his way here at this very moment."

"Yes, he might." Vary felt a little cheered by this idea. It was quite possible that Jeff would turn up on the doorstep one day unannounced or, as Thorne said, he'd gone off somewhere else for a week or two. Walking in the Lake District or Scotland, perhaps, which he loved to do, or sailing off the Cornish coast. There was no reason why he should answer to her, after all. He'd be in touch soon, she felt sure.

"Maybe he's got a girlfriend," Thorne remarked carelessly, swinging a stick at the brambles as he strolled along. He gave Vary a casual, sideways glance. "Being in love can make a man behave quite oddly, at times."

Vary shot him a swift look. There was an odd expression on his face and she felt her cheeks colour. "I don't think so," she said quickly. "I don't think that's the answer." And she turned away, conscious of her blush and furious with the betraying colour. What was there to blush about, after all – and why had Thorne had that quizzical expression on his face?

Why had she so swiftly denied the idea? There was no reason why Jeff shouldn't have a girlfriend, no reason at all. But it still seemed odd that he hadn't let her know.

Vary gave the bed a last pat and then turned away. Thorne was waiting in the other room ready to start work, and she was looking forward to it. Since beginning on this project, she'd become more and more interested in what Thorne was doing, and had asked him a number of questions about his work and life in India. It sounded gruelling but fascinating.

"I've always wanted to go to India," she said thoughtfully as they began work a few minutes later. "Some of my friends have been trekking in the Himalayas and that sounds marvellous. But it's the way of life I'm interested in as well as the fabulous scenery. And the languages, of course."

"And why do you find languages so interesting?" he asked.

"Oh, I don't know exactly. Their structure, and the way so many of them are linked together in their roots – the history of language itself is fascinating. But it's as much the fact that people need language to communicate. It's like learning an elaborate code. People are so separated by language differences and yet once they can talk to each other, they find they're not so very different after all."

"So you'd advocate one common language worldwide."

"Oh, I don't think so." She smiled at him. "I think it would be a great loss if we only had one language. All that richness gone, like reducing a complex tapestry to a grey canvas. No, I think we should all have a mother tongue and that they should all be preserved – but a common language, as well, to enable us all to communicate, yes, that's an ideal worth striving for."

"We're working that way though, surely. English is the language that seems to be taking over the world, despite the French and the Germans and Spanish who have spread their own languages. And yet English is suposed to be one of the most difficult languages to learn."

"The fact that it's the one most commonly used disproves that," Vary pointed out. "And other national-ities can often speak it better than we do ourselves! It's often the most concise, too – look at instruction manuals written in half a dozen different languages and see which one takes up most room and which the least." She laughed. "We seem to have come a long way from India! But I'd still like to go there one day, and not just to learn the language, either. It's people I'm really interested in – language is just the means of talking to each other. We have to be interested in each other first."

"And you're interested in people? How they live?" Thorne was looking at her intently.

"Yes. Yes, I am."

"Interested enough to want to help the less for-tunate?"

Vary frowned a little. "I think I could only go to a place like India on that basis. Not as a tourist, even though my Himalayan-trekking friends tell me that it helps the economy. I just wouldn't be able to feel easy, travelling like a rich person – even though I'm not, in European terms – through poverty. I'd have to be doing something useful to justify being there at all."

Thorne stared at her for a moment, then nodded and turned away. "Well, let's start doing something useful now, shall we? Those notes we did yesterday, I want to go through them again."

It was lunchtime before they paused for a rest, and Thorne stretched again, his broad body taut with muscle. Vary quickly looked away, aware that he would notice her slightest reaction, and got up to lead the way out for their midday bread and cheese. The sun was blazing down from a clear blue sky, and she slipped off her shirt and shorts and relaxed on the rough grass in her bikini, face lifted to the warmth.

"I thought we might go out for a meal tonight," Thorne remarked as he spread crusty French bread with creamy Brie and bit into it. "We've worked hard – we deserve a bit of relaxation. Especially you," he added, his eyes crinkling as he looked down at her. "You don't even get paid for it."

"I don't want to be paid," Vary said quickly. "I just want to help. But a meal sounds lovely," she added, thinking of the endless salads, cold meats and roast chickens they'd been living on for the past few days.

"I'd like that, so long as it doesn't offend against your principles."

Thorne stretched out a bare foot and nudged her in the ribs, his touch spreading like fire over her abdomen. "Don't tease. I can see you're never going to let me forget that *Boeuf à la Bourguignonne*. One of these days I shall take you to some really decadent restaurant, patronised by all the rich and famous parasites in the world, and force-feed you like a Strasbourg goose. Then you'll be sorry!"

"Try me," Vary said sleepily. "But they aren't all parasites, you know. Some of them work very hard, they just happen to earn a lot of money. Why not spend it? It gives other people employment."

"That's the theory, I know. I just can't bring myself to think that way." Thorne finished his bread and took another piece. "Good cooking I can appreciate. But I'd rather have a hearty peasant dish, brimming with things from the farmyard and the kitchen garden, than the most exotic creation in a Parisian restaurant. It isn't just the food, it's the whole atmosphere, the principle behind it. I suppose it all boils down to self-indulgence. I look at the people and imagine what they've done with their day: getting up at noon after last night's excesses, eating far too much lunch, probably spending money all afternoon on things they don't need, spending half the evening getting ready to go out again and then wining and dining away the night before staggering home to bed to sleep it off ready for the next day. I like to feel I've earned my meals. I like to feel I've a right to be eating them, a right to be alive."

Vary didn't answer. She could see and understand exactly what Thorne meant – but wasn't he taking it all a little too seriously? And on the heels of that thought came another – was it any surprise if he did, having seen what he'd seen and living the way he had?

They worked through the afternoon, finishing with another swim. This time, Vary didn't follow Thorne out into deep water; she stayed within her depth, swimming lazily under the hot sun, taking pleasure in the silky feel of the water washing gently over her skin, noting the increasing richness of her tan – a soft gold in comparison with Thorne's mahogany darkness. There was little risk of burning now, but she still smoothed a high-factor cream over herself before and after each swim and, when she came up the beach, her hair almost as black as Thorne's as it streamed down to her slender waist, the droplets gleamed on her skin like diamonds on honey-coloured satin.

Spreading her towel out on the sand, she stretched herself out on it, delighting in the feel of smooth, slim flesh over delicate bones. The warmth soaked into her body, relaxing muscles that were tired from sitting at a typewriter, lulling her into a languorous drowsiness, and her eyelids fluttered against the brightness. The soft rhythm of waves washing over the beach was like the rustle of autumn leaves in her ears, and she was only vaguely aware of the strident cries of gulls and the chug of a small fishing boat as it crossed the bay.

"Don't you *ever* learn?"

Thorne's voice jerked her awake and her eyelids snapped open. He was standing over her, magnificently posed with legs pillared apart, his torso like that of a Greek god as he bunched brown fists against his hips. The deep burgundy briefs he wore left little to the imagination – and they talk about *women* wearing revealing clothes, Vary thought, almost unable to keep her eyes from dwelling on the suggestion of burgeoning power. His eyes, when she finally met them, were laughing at her. Vary felt the colour deepen in her cheeks, knowing that he must have seen and understood every thought in her mind during her slow examination.

"You were falling asleep again," he accused her. "And having a tan already doesn't automatically render you immune to burning. This sun's hot, Vary, and the air is particularly clear and unpolluted. So let's not take any more risks, all right?"

"I'm not taking any risks." Vary rose lithely to her toes. She still had to look up at him, but at least she didn't feel as vulnerable as when lying at his feet. "But you're right – I *was* falling asleep. I've been feeling drowsy all day."

He glanced at her in concern as they walked back up the beach to the cottage. "You're all right, aren't you? Have I been working you too hard? Maybe you should take a day off."

"Oh, no!" Even as she hastily disclaimed the idea, Vary wondered what would have been her reaction if he'd said '*we* should take the day off'. "Not unless you want to yourself, anyway."

"No, not really," he said thoughtfully. "We're just in the middle of a tricky bit and I don't want to lose my train of thought. And if you don't mind continuing to help . . ."

"I don't mind at all. I'm enjoying it. Let's finish and then take time off, as you first suggested." She looked up at him, eyes luminous in the dimness as they entered the cottage. "We'll relax all the more for having done a good job."

Thorne stood quite still, looking down at her. His own eyes were dark with an emotion she hardly dared to acknowledge. For a moment – an aeon? – the whole world seemed to pause in its spinning. The trees, the grasses, the shrubs outside ceased to rustle in the breeze; the birds held their breath. And then Thorne took her very gently in his arms.

Her lips were already parted when he laid his own upon them, soft and willing. She felt her mouth shape itself to his as if they had been lovers for years, and she nestled into his arms as if she were coming home. Her own arms wound themselves around his neck, drawing him closer as she pressed her body against him. The contact of their skins brought a gasp from each of them; Vary was sharply aware of his contours, even as her own merged and moulded with them. She moved against him, breathless from the fire that scorched her limbs and burned its way up through her body to set her heart kicking like an untamed mare. From somewhere deep in Thorne's breast she felt a groan force its way into the open, and then his gentleness had vanished as passion took its place, his lips grew demanding, his hands urgent on her smooth, bare skin.

Vary twisted in his arms, panic and desire battling together. Her bones seemed to have melted away, leaving her pliant body without support, so that she had to cling to him or fall. Unfamilar and terrifying sensations were tearing at her heart, her blood was behaving like over-fermented wine as it surged through her veins, and her mind was a maelstrom of turbulent emotion. She wanted Thorne – oh, how she wanted him! – to continue, his passion unleashed at last from the tight control he'd been keeping over it during the past week. She wanted an even closer contact, to feel his skin against hers where now brief bikini and pants held them apart. She wanted to abandon herself completely to their matching desire, to feel his heart and body in unison with hers, to know that for just a little while he might love her.

And there, her mind brought her up with a jolt. Love! That was what it was all about, this quivering fire that blazed through her body, this urgent need for total submission. Love. It wasn't just chemistry or lust that she felt for this man who had been – was still – such an enigma to her. It was an emotion far deeper than physical desire, an emotion that went straight to the depths of her soul. It was love: total, irrevocable love. And once she had allowed it to reach its inevitable conclusion, she would be committed for the rest of her life.

And Thorne? Even as the thoughts fled through her mind, she knew that unless he felt the same emotion for her, there would be nothing but pain to follow. Pain, and a black, bottomless pit of despair. A pain she couldn't face.

With a gasp of pure terror, Vary twisted herself out of his arms. She was on the other side of the room before Thorne, shaking his head like a dazed bull, seemed to realise what had happened. At once, she was shot through with guilty dismay.

"I – I'm sorry, Thorne," she said jerkily, her voice ragged. "I didn't mean – it's not that I—" Words failed her and she raised a hand to brush away the tears of frustration. Well, there wouldn't be any danger from Thorne now, that was certain! No man would risk that kind of brush-off twice. If only, she thought miserably, there were some way of *explaining*. But she could never tell him what her true feelings were.

Thorne looked across at her, his eyes once more as veiled as a moonless night. His gaze rested on her for a long, long moment; then to her astonishment he gave a crooked grin and lifted one shoulder in a half-shrug.

"You don't have to apologise," he said, and his voice was only slightly jerky. "It was entirely my fault. Put it down to the sun – and proximity. It won't happen again." And he turned away and disappeared into his workroom, closing the door quietly behind him.

No, Vary thought, looking sadly at the door, I don't

believe it will. If ever a man had complete control over himself, it must be Thorne Moran.

She went slowly into her own room, feeling that she had just passed up the experience of the century.

Chapter Seven

The restaurant was small, with only half a dozen gingham-covered tables around its rough stone walls. There was a bottle of home-made wine on one side of each table, and a red glass jar with a candle flickering in it on the other side. A small pot of flowers brightened the centre. The welcoming warmth of the atmosphere was completed by the large fire built on a brick plinth across the end of the room, with a grill placed over it on which the burly *patron* was already cooking some steaks.

"Very nice indeed," Thorne commented as they sat down. "You've been here before?"

"With Jeff." She nodded, and missed the way his eyes momentarily darkened. "There are lots of these village restaurants around this area, of course, and they're all good, but this was our favourite." She smiled as the *patron* finished his cooking and carried the laden plates to another table before coming across to them. *"Bonsoir,* Maurice."

"Mademoiselle Varee!" There was no mistaking the delighted recognition that spread across his swarthy face, and Vary wondered ruefully why she'd never thought of bringing Thorne here to prove her identity. Well, it didn't matter now. "It is a long time, too long, since you 'ave been to see us. And where is the cousin? Monsieur Jeff." As always, he managed to make Jeff's name sound as if it had an 'h' in it; he had never, in spite of many hilarious lessons, mastered the true English sound.

"Jeff's in England – he teaches, you remember. But this is Monsieur Moran, a friend of his, who's staying in the cottage." The liquid eyes turned to Thorne and examined him, as if assessing his worthiness to be using Jeff's cottage. "Monsieur Moran likes local foods," Vary went on hastily, wondering what Thorne was making of this appraisal. "What do you recommend, Maurice?"

"Ah!" The dark face beamed. "What should I *not* recommend, Mademoiselle Varee? *All* my dishes are good! But for a beginner, you must of course 'ave the shellfish, *assiette des fruits de mer*, or at least the oysters. And to follow – *bien*, there is the *homard à l'armoricain*, or if you do not wish for two fishes, we 'ave *gigot d'agneau*, which comes from the Breton sheep, or we 'ave—" he flung up his hands and rolled his eyes. "But it is *all* good. Look at the *menu gastronomique* and see for yourself. It is almost enough simply to feast the eyes!"

He handed them a menu. Smiling, Vary bent her head close to Thorne's to read it, and caught the tang of fresh aftershave. There was something else, too, a subtle male scent that she was coming to recognise as uniquely his, and which disturbed her more every time she noticed it. Taking a deep breath to control the sudden quiver that shook her, she concentrated on the menu.

"Maurice is right," she said, "it's almost enough just to sit here and read it! And a lot less fattening." She glanced up, suddenly anxious. "This doesn't go against your principles?"

"I'd be a fool to come to France if it did," he said ruefully. "I'd forgotten just how important food is in this country! But maybe it's a good thing to be reminded. You're right, Vary, there isn't a thing wrong with eating good food, well prepared. It gives pleasure as well as sustenance, and it's not necessarily self-indulgence. It adds to the quality of life."

"The quality you say is important to us all," she said, and he nodded.

"What's the use of trying to haul people out of the rice-bowl stage when there's nothing better to offer them, when we've all been reduced to the same grim standard? No, I'll go back to India refreshed and with a new awareness of life – an awareness that will help me to help them. At least, that's the way I hope it'll be."

"You're going back, then?" Vary felt a strange pang as he nodded again.

"I'll be going back, yes. There was never any doubt of that." His eyes seemed to hold some kind of message for her as he turned their raking glance on her face, a message she wasn't sure she wanted to understand. "My life's out there, Vary," he said quietly, "nothing is going to change that."

Maurice was at their sides again, but not to hurry them over their order – as Vary knew, no French *patron* ever did that. He merely wanted to know if they would like an aperitif, "On the 'ouse," he assured them, his smile widening under the bushy moustache, and Vary felt warmed by his obvious affection.

"I'd love one," she declared. "Kir, please." The mixture of *cassis* and white wine had always been her favourite, and when it came she sipped it with pleasure. Thorne, too, tasted his drink with enjoyment. It was almost, she thought, as if he had thrown off his gravity like a cloak, revealing an unexpectedly light-hearted self underneath. And from the moment their drinks arrived, the evening steadily improved.

They both had *assiette des fruits de mer*, gazing at the huge platter with awe when it arrived, hardly daring to spoil its beautiful symmetry. In the centre lay a huge crab, its shell replaced to cover the delicious dressed meat inside, its legs carefully arranged around its body and spread out over the assortment of other shellfish – oysters with shells big enough to carry a bar of soap, mussels drenched in white wine, cockles, winkles and langoustines that looked more like baby lobsters. An array of strange-looking implements came with the platter, each one designed to deal with a different shellfish, and Vary knew from experience that it would take them well over half an hour to clear the plate. She remembered her first experience of this Breton dish and smiled. Maurice had come out to see how she was getting along just as she had laid down her last utensil. With a cry of horror, he had made it very clear that she hadn't finished at all, but had left all the best parts still in their shells, and seizing an implement that looked more like a weapon of war than an eating utensil, he had shown her how to extract every last, delicious morsel – and had stood over her to see that she did so!

"I worked out once that the whole thing comes to only about a hundred calories," she told Thorne as they plied their prongs and needles. "And with the energy you use in getting at it all, you must lose weight! Not that I'd care if you didn't, it's so delicious. And all gathered up from the beach at low tide," she added wickedly.

"It's marvellous." Thorne lifted a particularly succulent langoustine. "I'd say Jeff doesn't know what he's missing, but I guess he does."

"Oh, Jeff doesn't like it," Vary said cheerfully. "He used to have just a bowl of soup. I felt sorry for him sometimes, having to wait for me to chew my way through all these things – but I was never sorry enough to have a bowl of soup too! Breton soup's marvellous, of course, especially Maurice's, but it could never compare with this."

She felt Thorne watching her as she ate, but for once his regard didn't embarrass her. Perhaps it was the *kir*, she thought hazily, combined with the wine in which the mussels had been cooked; or perhaps they were simply getting past the stage of being embarrassed by each other. Not that Thorne had ever been embarrassed by *her*, he was far too self-contained to allow such a thing. She smiled at him, unfeigned enjoyment lighting her face, and was rewarded by a lifting of his own rather sombre features. Her heart kicked suddenly. She'd been right at that first meeting, he *was* damned attractive! And a wave of sheer longing swept across her and caused her to look away quickly, in case he saw and understood.

For their main course they both had *sole meunière*, knowing that delicious though Maurice's special dishes might be, the simple ones were likely to be the best. Vary had declared herself unable to cope with lobster after the assortment of shellfish she had already eaten, and Thorne agreed with her. He chose a bottle of muscadet to accompany the fish and poured her a generous glass.

"You'll have to carry me home," she remarked, admiring the pale straw colour of the wine, glowing like another lamp in the candlelight. "I'd forgotten the effect *kir* has on me."

"And what's that?" he asked, his eyes as dark as the sky outside, with twin stars sparkling somewhere in their depths. Vary felt trapped; enmeshed in their burning grip. With an effort she dropped her own gaze and took a deep breath.

"I don't quite know," she said shakily. "It usually relaxes me – makes me feel happy and contented, as if nothing can ever go wrong again. But tonight . . ."

"Something can go wrong?" he persisted, and she

lifted her eyes again and met his with a bewildered candour that hid nothing. Unable to answer, she shook her head helplessly, and Thorne reached out and took the hand that lay between them on the table.

"Nothing will go wrong," he said gently, and turned her palm upwards, tracing a line on it with his finger that seemed to flame its way directly into Vary's heart. "Don't worry, little one, nothing will go wrong." And he lifted her hand and kissed it.

Vary ate the rest of her meal in a daze. She barely noticed the *crêpes* filled with early strawberries that Maurice set before them, and picked out her cheese from the large platter almost as if she didn't care about it, only paying any attention at all because she knew Maurice's feelings would be hurt otherwise. The muscadet sang in her brain and filled her veins with sunlight. She felt elated, excited – and scared. And Thorne's closeness grew more intoxicating with every moment, his magnetism a constant and almost tangible presence between them, or was it just him? Was it more a quality that had sprung up between them, that chemistry she'd once acknowledged simmering away like a pot about to boil over . . . ? Vary shivered, suddenly terrified. Oh Thorne, Thorne, she wanted to cry, what are you doing to me? What's going to happen?

They left the restaurant at last, Vary conscious of Maurice's beaming face, good wishes and exhortations to return; but more acutely conscious of Thorne's hand under her arm. She was glad of it, too; the fresh air reminded her of the powerful effect of *kir*, especially when followed with muscadet and a good meal. She stopped by Thorne's car, standing close to him as he unlocked the door; and then, without being aware of any movement, she was in his arms, lifting her mouth to his.

"Oh, God, Vary," he muttered thickly, and then his mouth covered hers, hungry, devouring. His tongue flicked against hers, then probed more surely, more desperately, and Vary responded without reserve, straining against him, conscious of nothing but the meeting of tongues, teeth, lips and hearts. She felt Thorne's strong, sensitive hands slide down her body, moulding her curves, pressing her hips to his, and a small gasp escaped her as she felt the swell of his desire. As she moved against him, one hand moved up to cup a breast that was suddenly taut, while his other hand moved sensuously over her thigh. Her own frantic whimpers matched his groans, and she was sure they must both be deafened by the roar of her blood, the thunder of her heart. Briefly, she remembered that they were in a dark corner of the square, the car deep in the shadow of an overhanging tree. But if they had been floodlit, she wouldn't have cared. She wanted only to be here, in Thorne's arms, pouring out her heart to his, showering him with her love.

This time, the word didn't jolt her away from him. It didn't matter any more whether Thorne loved her or not, whether there might be pain at the end of this encounter. All that mattered was the here and now: the fact that she loved him; the fact that tonight she would give herself without constraint. If he left her tomorrow, she would at least have that. And if she never loved again – and she knew, deep down, that she never would – she would for this brief spell have loved more than most women loved in a lifetime.

"This is no good," Thorne muttered roughly. "Get into the car, Vary, for God's sake. Let's get back to the cottage."

Vary left his arms and slid into the passenger seat. She didn't want to leave the warmth of his body, didn't want to stop even for a moment, but she knew that what he said made sense. They couldn't make love in a village square; they had to go back. And it was only ten minutes' drive.

Thorne accomplished that drive in something between six minutes and seven, driving as grimly and purpose-fully as if he were going to save lives. He drove with one hand on the wheel, holding Vary's hand closely in the other, keeping it pressed hard against his thigh. He didn't look at her as he drove, and he didn't speak. And she didn't want him to. Nothing must break the spell.

They arrived at the track that led to the cottage gate, where Thorne normally parked his car. He swung into the narrow opening, his headlamps flooding the old stone walls with harsh light, and slammed on his brakes.

There was another car already standing at the gate. A long, low, glossy car that looked both exclusive and expensive. And out of it, as they both stared in

117

disbelief, stepped an equally expensive-looking woman, her ash-blonde hair lit into sunlight by the blaze of the lamps.

Thorne muttered something and slid out of his seat, with Vary following. A heavy lump of dread had settled itself deep in her stomach. She looked at the woman, taking in the details of the soft, white fur jacket, the close-fitting dress that looked like real silk and moved with a sensuous ripple over her perfect figure as she came towards them. And she closed her eyes. Had she really believed that nothing could go wrong?

"Thorne, darling!" The voice was a soft, husky purr just as Vary had known it must be. "You've no idea what a job I've had to track you down. However did you find this incredibly rural place?" She came right into Thorne's arms and lifted her golden face for a kiss that seemed to Vary to go on for much too long. "Never mind, I'm here now. And just in time, it seems. You know, you really are a *very* naughty boy – but I suppose I mustn't blame you." She looked past him at Vary, standing there feeling dazed and sick with apprehension. "*Allez-vous-en, ma petite. Monsieur Moran ne vous veut pas. Je suis Madame Moran. Comprenez-vous?*"

Vary drew in a sharp breath. This woman had taken her for a village girl, brought home for the night, presumably to satisfy Thorne's masculine needs! But, worse than that, she was saying, in execrable French, that she was Thorne's *wife*!

His wife! It had never occurred to her that he might be married. With a stifled cry of dismay and self-disgust, she turned and ran into the night, ignoring Thorne's call and the laughter of the woman who was in his arms.

Where she was going, she had no idea. But it wasn't back to the cottage. The way she felt now, she could never go there again.

Chapter Eight

Vary woke heavy-eyed, her head muzzy and her brain sluggish. She lay quite still for a few moments, looking around the room and wondering what to do next.

Her flight from the cottage last night hadn't taken her very far, only down to the beach, where she'd stopped and sat down on a boulder, dizzy with wine and shock. She covered her face with her hands, trying not to hear the soft noises of the night, wanting to drown herself in her misery. Oh, how could she have let herself be so deceived? Thorne, *married*! And his wife, that glittering blonde, arriving on the doorstep just when Vary was about to throw away all her pride, all her self-control and spend the night with him, making love, committing herself to him. Committing herself, she thought in anguish, to a lifetime of pain and regret.

It had never occurred to her to ask if he were married. Nothing he had ever said or done had suggested that he was. And if he were, she would never have dreamed that it could be to a woman like that fur-clad blonde, a woman who clearly expected a great deal of money to be spent on her, a woman who would enjoy everything Thorne had affected to despise – high living, exotic food and drink, a constant supply of new and fashionable clothes. It didn't seem possible. But the woman's words had been plain enough. There was no escaping the meaning of that schoolgirl French.

Vary sighed and lifted her tear-drowned face. The sky was a canopy of deep black velvet, spangled with a silver dust of stars. There was no moon, but the sea was lit with a fluorescence that shimmered on the gently shifting water, a coverlet of platinum-pale shot-silk. The tiny waves were edged with a foam as delicate as Maltese lace, like the deliberate showing of an embroidered petticoat, and around the shores there were a few lights, glowing like lanterns in the clear air.

Only minutes ago, the beauty had been an enhancement of her mood, lifting her to the anticipation of ecstasy in Thorne's arms. Now, it was a knife to her heart, stabbing her with its unfeeling cruelty.

"Vary! *Vary!*"

Thorne's voice sounded close to her, so close that she couldn't repress a tiny cry of shock. Immediately, he was at her side, holding her in arms that were like iron as she struggled against them. Frantically, she twisted and turned, unable to do more than pound his rock-like chest with small, ineffectual fists. She could feel his body, rigid with anger, pressed hard against hers and even in her turmoil she couldn't ignore the effect it had on her, the flame of desire that shot between them as they came into closer, more intimate, contact. Tears of humiliation streamed down her cheeks as she realised that even now she wasn't immune, that she probably never would be, and that to Thorne, she must have been no more than a passing entertainment, a girl who would be easy to seduce and as easy to leave behind.

"Vary, stop it! Stop fighting me – it's doing no good. We've got to talk. Calm down, for God's sake."

"Talk?" she spat at him. "What have we got to talk about? The fact that you're married? That you had a wife and never bothered to tell me? Or maybe you just forgot – after all, you've had a lot on your mind lately, haven't you? And I can quite see that a wife who looked like that *would* be easy to forget!"

"Vary, *stop*! You don't know what you're talking about. It isn't like that at all—"

"Isn't it? So just what *is* it like?" Vary glared up at him, her eyes two black pits of anger in the pallor of her face. "Tell me, I'm fascinated."

Thorne sighed. He looked almost gaunt in this light, she thought, haggard as if life had suddenly become too much for him. Well, maybe it had, but whose fault was that? He obviously hadn't expected his wife to turn up just at that moment – hadn't expected her to come here at all, from what she'd said – but he must have known it was possible.

Fleetingly, Vary wondered just what their relationship was. It was almost as if he'd been hiding from her, yet there'd been no mistaking the nature of that kiss. And his lips had still been warm from her own

. . . Humiliation squirmed through her again and she closed her eyes, fighting the tears.

"Look, Vary," Thorne said gently, "if you'll only listen to me I'll explain. I know how you must be feeling—"

"Oh, do you?" she broke in bitterly. "I wonder how you think you know that. Did someone do this to you once – promise everything and then be unable to give anything? Did—"

"I've never promised you a thing, Vary," Thorne said quietly, and she was silenced. He hadn't, it was true – not in so many words. But the way he'd looked at her, the way he'd touched and kissed her hand in the restaurant, the way he'd begun to make love to her the moment they were outside, wasn't all that a promise, of a kind?

"I didn't mean you'd promised me anything tangible," she said shakily. "But you made it quite clear what you expected."

"And so did you." His voice was still quiet, reasonable. "You weren't fighting me then, Vary."

Suddenly, the tension drained out of her, leaving her feeling flat and exhausted. She felt herself go limp in his arms, and after a moment's hesitation he relaxed his iron grip. Vary stood quietly, still encircled but knowing she could walk away any moment if she chose.

"All right," she said wearily, "tell me. If you think it will make any difference."

Thorne looked down at her. His face was sombre in the dim light, shadowed with more than the night's darkness. He sighed again and shook his head. "I must have been mad, letting things build up like that between us," he said. "You're so damned vulnerable – I should have known better."

"Just tell me," she said, flinching away from his words. If there was one thing she didn't want, it was pity!

Thorne nodded. "Yes. Well, first of all, Zelah *isn't* my wife. That just wasn't true, Vary, and I was just as horrified to hear her say it as you were."

"Not your wife?" For the second time that evening, the world swayed. "But – I don't understand. Why should she say a thing like that, if it wasn't true?"

Thorne shrugged. "To warn you off, I suppose. She obviously thought you were some village maiden, brought home for the night's entertainment and picked on that as the quickest way of getting rid of you. She may also have been thinking of the local reaction to my sharing the cottage with her, I suppose."

Vary doubted that. The blonde – what was it he'd called her? – hadn't struck her at all as the type who might worry about the proprieties, especially those of a remote Breton village. But there was something more immediately worrying in what Thorne had just said.

"Sharing the cottage? You mean she's *staying* here?"

"That's her idea, yes. Vary, I'd better tell you something about Zelah. Zelah Tobitt is her full name and I've known her for quite a while." He hesitated. "To you, she might have looked like someone who'd never done a day's work in her life – unless it was modelling for something like *Vogue*. In fact, she's a brilliant chemist. She works in a laboratory in Kent and we've done quite a lot together."

I bet you have, Vary thought cynically, and not all of it in the lab. Aloud, she said, "A chemist? Is she working on your new drug, then?"

"That's right. We've been collaborating on quite a lot of the tests. As you know, all the lab work was done some time ago – you've been helping me type up the reports and the paper – and when I came over here to do the paperwork, I didn't leave my address. Deliberately, because I didn't want any distractions."

"And Zelah's a distraction," Vary suggested. "Yes, I can quite see that."

Thorne sighed again. "Look, what happened in my private life before I met you is none of your business, Vary. I'm a man, as you were only too pleased to acknowledge yourself not so long ago, and Zelah's an attractive woman. Yes, she'd have been a distraction, or so I thought." He gave her an irritable glance. "She wouldn't have been any more so than you, I may say."

"Thank you for nothing!" Vary snapped, her own annoyance matching his. "All right, Thorne, you've explained. Zelah's not your wife but she's just about everything else. Let's leave it at that, shall we?"

Thorne stared at her, then shrugged. "That suits me," he said curtly. "And now we'll go back to the cottage." He took her arm in a hard grip and began to lead her along the beach.

Vary hung back. "No, Thorne. I don't want to go to the cottage. Playing gooseberry's never been my style and—"

"Oh, for God's sake!" he snapped. "Where on earth do you suppose you could go at this time of night? Grow up, Vary, Zelah's not going to eat you. I've explained who you are."

"Oh, you have? And just what was going on when we came back to the cottage? She must have loved that!"

"And I've explained that you've been helping me with the work," he went on, ignoring her outburst. "She understands all that. And I doubt if you'll even see her tonight anyway – she was very tired when she arrived and she'd been waiting outside the cottage for quite a while. She's probably gone to bed by now."

Vary stopped dead. "Gone to bed? And just which bed do you suppose she'll have gone to?"

"I've no idea, and quite frankly I don't care." Thorne gave her arm a painful yank. "Come on, Vary. We'll find out where Zelah is when we get there, and we'll just have to sort ourselves out as best we can. So accept that, will you, and stop behaving like a child."

Vary allowed him to drag her back up the beach and along the narrow path. Tamarisk branches brushed their soft leaves against her face, as if in comfort. But for her there was no comfort in the beauty of the night. By now, she and Thorne would have been together in that big bed, making love – and she honestly didn't know whether she was glad or sorry that they weren't.

All she did know was that the moment had passed. It

was unlikely ever to come again. And meanwhile, she was left with a heart that still burned hopelessly with a love that would never be quenched.

Zelah, they discovered, had taken over the big double bed by the time they reached the cottage. The door was firmly closed and Thorne gave Vary a wry glance.

"That seems to be a fait accompli," he observed. "You'd better have the other one."

"No, I'll take the settee," Vary said dully. "It's much too small for you and I was quite comfortable there. Perhaps she won't be staying long." She didn't have much confidence in that, though. Zelah Tobitt hadn't struck her as the kind of woman who would go off leaving her lover – and Thorne had virtually admitted that that was what he was – sharing a cottage with another girl. She prepared for bed, wondering just how long Thorne would occupy the small bed before moving in with Zelah. Well, it hardly mattered. What she had to decide was what to do next. She couldn't stay here, that was obvious.

But she still hadn't made up her mind in the morning. Her brain dull with hours of wakefulness followed by a too-heavy sleep, she lay staring at the cottage walls, too bemused to think clearly at all. It was only gradually that the sounds from outside permeated her consciousness.

Voices in the garden, she thought hazily. They were having breakfast out there together, Thorne and Zelah. Sharing croissants and coffee – yes, she could smell it now – just as she and Thorne had shared them. She wondered if they had also shared an early-morning swim and doubted it, Zelah's shining blonde hair looked too carefully arranged to take kindly to salt water. But someone must have gone to the village for the rolls. Perhaps they had walked along the lane together, enjoying the fresh scents of the morning, listening to the symphony of the birds.

Already, Vary was beginning to feel more than slightly redundant. She must get away from here, she thought unhappily. It was time to start her travels again. But somehow, the thought had lost its appeal.

Whoever had gone to the village for croissants had brought enough for three, and there were several left in the basket when Vary made her appearance. Aware that she couldn't hope to compete with Zelah's sophisticated glamour, she had slipped into her usual shirt and shorts, feeling dowdy and quite unconscious of the fact that her slim figure, with its small, neat breasts and long, slender legs, needed little to add to its charm. Arms and legs were the same honey-brown as her face, and the swathe of soft, mahogany hair brought out the liquid darkness of her eyes. But Vary was too accustomed to these things to notice them and as she came slowly out through the door she could see only the fashionable cut of Zelah's scarlet linen dress, with its crossover front emphasising the voluptuous curve of her full breasts, while pulling in closely to fit her small waist.

Zelah was laughing at something Thorne had said, her head tilted back to show the arch of her long neck, lips parted to reveal small, white teeth. She turned slightly as Vary came into view, and her fine brows lifted, the baby-blue eyes widening in amusement.

"Why, here she is, your little amanuensis! How cool you look, Vary my sweet – and you're so right not to bother about dressing, in these parts. Unfortunately," she sighed extravagantly, glancing down at her own perfectly-dressed figure, "I brought *all* the wrong clothes for a country holiday. But then, I didn't realise when I set off just how deep in rural bliss Thorne had buried himself."

Vary said nothing, there didn't seem to be anything to say. She slid into the third chair and poured herself some coffee. She didn't look at Thorne at all, but she was nerve-tinglingly aware of his presence.

"I really must apologise for upsetting you last night," Zelah went on, laying a red-tipped finger on Vary's bare arm. Vary looked down at it with the feeling she might have had if a scorpion had suddenly touched her with its claws. "I simply didn't realise who you were. Well, how could I? I thought Thorne was being a naughty boy and bringing home one of the village girls, not that one could blame him, of course, it's simply ages since we were together and he's a very masculine man, don't you agree?"

There was something more than mere cattiness in that last little question, Vary thought, looking at the avid face. Zelah was asking her something, asking whether she and Thorne had slept together. And at the same

129

time, implying that if they had it was only because Zelah wasn't around to satisfy him.

"Most men are quite masculine, aren't they?" she said noncommittally. "At least, most of the ones I've met have been. But you've probably met far more than I have." She took a croissant and split it open.

Zelah's face darkened, but she kept the bright smile securely pinned to her face. "Oh, I expect I have," she agreed carelessly. "After all, I do move in rather exceptional circles. You've had quite a sheltered upbringing, it seems, from what Thorne tells me."

Vary shot Thorne a furious look. How dared he tell this woman about her? Not that there was anything in her history to be ashamed of – but all the same, for Thorne to take it upon himself to tell Zelah the things she'd told him was really a bit much.

Thorne returned her look imperturbably, and she bit her lip and spread jam on her croissant. This was going to be an impossible situation, she thought angrily, and decided that the sooner it was ended, the better. But what about Thorne's work? She'd promised to stay until it was finished, and she couldn't go back on that. Not simply because it was a promise to Thorne – she might quite easily have broken it in that case – but because, in a strange sort of way, it was a promise made to all those thousands of people in India and other countries, people who were waiting for his new miracle drug, whose lives depended upon it. People who might die if it were held up for one second longer than necessary.

"By the way," Zelah said, breaking in on her thoughts

with uncanny accuracy, "you won't need to do any more of that boring typing you've been so kindly helping Thorne with. Not now I'm here. You can go on with your holiday – it was to have a break from your travelling that you came here, wasn't it?" She smiled charmingly. "Well, you carry on and enjoy yourself, sunbathing and swimming. And maybe Thorne will lend you his car to do some sightseeing. You wouldn't mind Vary driving your little rattletrap, would you, Thorne?"

Vary didn't give Thorne a chance to answer. She turned her head and looked him straight in the eye. "But what about your typing? Is – is Miss Tobitt going to do that?"

"Zelah, please," Zelah said, and Thorne, looking more uncomfortable than Vary had ever seen him, muttered, "Well, that's the general idea. It's quite a good one too, Vary. After all, Zelah knows the work, she won't be thrown by unfamiliar words, she's accustomed to my handwriting. She has a professional interest too, since she worked on many of the tests. And I can't impose on you any more, you've been marvellous and helped tremendously, but this *was* supposed to be your holiday and I quite agree with Zelah, you ought to be allowed to enjoy it." For the first time since Vary had known him, he refused to meet her eyes.

Vary stared at him. He was embarrassed – Thorne Moran, embarrassed! It was almost unbelievable. Not that he didn't have good reason to be, she thought

131

grimly. Kicking her aside like that, as if she were a worn-out glove. Well, she didn't have to stick around here to cause embarrassment for anyone, and she didn't have to put up with Zelah's barely concealed spite either.

"That's fine, then," she said, her tight voice betraying how hurt she really was. "I must admit I was getting rather tired of it all. But now that you've got Miss – Zelah – to do it for you, I can certainly get on with my holiday. Only I shan't be spending it here, thank you very much. I'll move on, find somewhere else to bask in the sun. Two's company, you know, and it's a very small cottage."

Something like dismay darkened Thorne's eyes then, but Vary was too high on her inner fury to take any notice. She regretted her words momentarily when she saw the quick triumph on Zelah's face, but hardened her determination. There was no future for her in staying here, only pain and humiliation. So it was best to get out, fast, and thank her lucky stars that Zelah had come along last night and not today. By today, she would have committed herself. As it was, there was a chance – wasn't there? – that she might one day recover.

"That sounds the most sensible thing you could do," Zelah purred. She shot a glance at Thorne. "Doesn't it, Thorne darling? Vary's obviously had enough of drugs and diseases, she can go on and enjoy her long holiday, while we carry on with the work. It really *is* important," she added, turning back to Vary. "But of course, one does need rather high qualifications to understand it."

"Does one? I would have thought most people could understand the horror of disease, and the need to find a cure." Vary glanced again at Thorne. "I'll get my things together straight after breakfast. You don't need to worry about me. I know this area pretty well, and I can easily find somewhere to stay while I decide what to do next."

His voice, when he spoke at last, was husky, almost as it had been when he was making love to her last night. "But you can't go yet, Vary," he said. "You've got to stay here for a while at least." His eyes were brilliant, reflecting the sky above, and Vary gazed at him in astonishment. Surely he wasn't *pleading* with her!

"Why not? What is there to stop me?" she paused, adding icily, "I'm sure *you* don't want me to stay, Thorne. Not now that you've got Zelah, who can do so much more for you than I can."

He sighed, then said flatly, "I rang Jeff while I was in the village this morning – just to let him know everything was all right. He's been ill, Vary – a nasty dose of flu, turning to pleurisy. His doctor has advised a complete rest for the remainder of the school term, and as soon as he's fit to travel he's coming over. He wants you to be here. And I think you should be."

So that was it. Thorne himself didn't care whether she stayed or went. Zelah wanted her to go, and as quickly as possible – a quick look at her face, sulky with this latest news, confirmed that. And Vary herself wanted nothing more than to be out of it, away from Thorne and his glamorous mistress and his overwhelmingly disturbing presence.

But there was no way she could go now, with Jeff ill and wanting her to be here. She would have to stay, watching Thorne and Zelah together, unable to do anything useful, unable to relax and enjoy herself. Unable to begin the long, painful and probably impossible process of getting Thorne out of her mind, her blood and her heart.

Trapped – she was more surely trapped than ever before.

Chapter Nine

M oodily, Vary took her things down to the beach and spread them in her accustomed place. Towel, rug, bag containing suntan lotion and the moisturiser which was almost the only make-up she used, book, writing-paper, a couple of rolls filled with cheese and tomato and a bottle of mineral water. It was a long, lonely day on the beach, but better than going back to the cottage for lunch and watching Thorne and Zelah emerge after a morning's work – though from the sleek complacency Zelah so often presented, Vary wondered more than once whether it had been work they had been engaged on during those quiet hours.

So far, she hadn't taken up Thorne's offer to use his car to go sightseeing. For some reason, she didn't want to stray far from the cottage. It was almost a masochistic streak in her, she thought, wanting to stay around the scene where she'd been hurt so badly. But it was as if there were an invisible cord, binding her to the place where Thorne was, allowing her to go so far and no farther. Like a dog on a long tether, she was brought up short if she tried to go beyond range.

Still, it was pleasant enough here and she was certainly getting enough rest. There was nothing for her to do now except the cooking, which she did just for something to do. She made daily trips into the village to buy fresh food, and had once been to the ancient town of Auray, where she had spent the day wandering around the narrow, picturesque streets of the St Goustan quarter, finding the house once stayed in by Benjamin Franklin and coming home laden with items not available in the small village supermarket.

That was the only excursion she had made. Since then, she'd been content to spend her time on the beach, reading the paperbacks she'd bought in Auray to improve her French, and swimming alone in the cool, salt sea.

Until this morning. This morning, it seemed she was to have company.

Vary had noticed the young Englishman once or twice before. She'd seen him in the village when she'd been buying croissants in the morning, and had returned his smile absently. She'd seen him again down by the little harbour, watching the fishermen, and this time had noticed his bright, fair hair, and diffident smile. But she still hadn't paid much attention and hadn't encouraged his rather tentative approach.

Now, he was sitting on the beach only fifty or so yards away from her, and as she spread her belongings around her and settled down on her rug she saw him glance up and give her a little half-wave. Vary hesitated, then waved back. You couldn't pretend not to see someone, when you were the only people in a small cove. And there wasn't much she could do about it when he got up and came over, evidently wanting to talk. In any case, she was bored and lonely. It might be quite pleasant to have someone else to talk to – someone to take her mind off Thorne and Zelah.

"Hello," the young man said, stopping a few yards away from her. "I hope you don't mind my speaking to you – only you seem to be on your own too, and I wondered if you knew this area."

"Yes, fairly well." Vary watched him uncertainly. Did he really want to know, or was this just a pick-up? Well, what if it was? People had to say something to start a conversation. "I've been coming here for some years with my cousin – he owns a cottage just back there, at the top of the beach." She waved a hand to where the cottage was hidden behind the broom and tamarisk.

"Oh, really? Is he with you now? I mean—" He stopped, then went on shyly, "Well, I've seen you several times and you always seem to be on your own."

"I am, virtually. Not in the cottage. Jeff – that's my cousin – isn't here, but there's a friend of his, using it to do some work in. And his—" she hesitated "—secretary. That's why I'm always on my own, I just do the cooking and so on."

"That doesn't sound much of a holiday," he said warmly, and sat down nearby.

"Oh, it's not bad. I only cook the evening meal and Thorne doesn't like elaborate meals so that makes it easy for me." She was beginning to like this young man. He was friendly and easy to talk to, his diffidence a restful change from Thorne's total confidence in himself. She looked at him more attentively, liking the openness of his face, the cheerful smile and warm hazel eyes.

"Thorne? That's an unusual name."

"Mm, it is. Perhaps his parents knew just how prickly he'd be," Vary said, and he joined in her laughter. It was good to laugh again, she discovered, realising just how long it was since she had done so with any enjoyment. Thorne had a dry wit which elicited smiles rather than laughter, and although Zelah laughed quite a lot it was never at anything that Vary thought in the least funny. Frequently, it was at Vary herself; Zelah seemed to get quite a lot of pleasure in pointing out any minor mistakes or pecadilloes, until Vary began to feel decidedly small.

"So you're not having all that good a holiday," he observed, and Vary found she couldn't contradict him. "Well, I've been a bit let down too. I was supposed to meet some friends here and they just haven't materialised. They'll be along sometime, but meanwhile I'm at a loose end."

His eyes were bright as he glanced sideways at her. "Look – tell me to push off if you like, but why don't we team up for a while? See a few sights, do some swimming, some exploring, whatever you like. I've never been to these parts before, so you can show me around a bit. That's if you'd like to."

"Well . . ." Vary looked quickly at him, then back at the sea. "I don't know . . ." What would Thorne say, she wondered, if she announced that she was going out with a stranger she'd met on the beach? And hard on the heels of that thought came two others: would he even care, and why should she tell him anyway? He wasn't her keeper! "It might be rather nice," she said cautiously, and he grinned.

"That's marvellous! Look – I haven't even introduced myself. I'm Gil Mitchell. University graduate, at present unemployed and seeing Europe while the situation gets sorted out. Had a windfall from an aunt which will keep me going through the summer and thought I might as well use it this way as sit at home waiting for it to dwindle until I need to draw Social Security. You?"

"Vary Carmichael. I'm seeing Europe, too. My grandfather left me some money with the instructions that this was the way it should be spent. He always wanted to bring me himself, but he was never fit enough." Vary smiled at him, thinking how similar their backgrounds must be. And he was more or less the same age as her, too – that made quite a change from Thorne's confident maturity, which scared her at times. *And* Zelah's poised sophistication. She felt her tension lessening as she took the hand Gil held out and shook it warmly.

"Well, so there we are. We know all about each other now." His grin was infectious, and she smiled back. "What shall we do first?"

"Well, I was planning to spend the day here, on the beach—" Vary began, but he interrupted her at once.

"That won't do! You've spent nearly every day this week on the beach – yes, I've seen you." He gave her a disarming glance. "It's time you got out and about. What is there to see?"

"Well, there are the standing stones. If you're interested in prehistory – not everyone is."

"I'm prepared to be interested in anything. What are these standing stones, anyway? Sort of Stonehenge?"

"Yes, a similar kind of thing." Vary described the stones of Carnac as she'd described them to Thorne, and was gratified by Gil's attention. "It's a bit too late to go there today," she said, glancing at her watch. "But we could go over on the ferry and see the tumulus on Gavrinis. And we could walk over to the little island – the tide's low all afternoon so it won't be any good for swimming."

"Sounds a good programme." Gil scrambled to his feet and held out his hand. "Come on then, collect up all your things and we'll start. You can drop them in at the cottage – I'll wait on the beach."

"All right." Vary was quite glad he didn't suggest accompanying her to the cottage. Explaining him to Thorne and Zelah was something that could wait until later. She hurried back along the track, slipping quietly into the little kitchen to collect some extra rolls and cheese, and then tiptoed out. There was no sound from the workroom; not even the clack of the typewriter.

Well, it was none of her business if Thorne and Zelah spent half the morning in bed together. There wasn't any reason in the world why she should care what they did.

And she ran back down the path, smiling gaily at Gil, ready to enjoy her day out in his company.

If nothing else, he would help her to pass the time until Jeff arrived.

The day passed more pleasantly than Vary had dared hope. Gil Mitchell was exactly the right companion for a holiday, she thought as they lay on the grassy bank of the little island, above the beach. Clearly no historian, he'd nevertheless shown a light-hearted interest in the tumulus, following Vary through the dim passages and listening as she explained the various features. Afterwards, they had come back to the mainland and then walked around the point to where the causeway led across to the small, green island where the convent stood.

"You can only cross at low tide," Vary commented as they picked their way across seaweed-draped rocks. "We'll have to be careful not to get cut off. But it's so pleasant over here – see the notice, asking visitors to observe the convent's request for peace and quiet. It seems to have a different atmosphere from the mainland, peaceful though that is."

They wandered along the path that led round the edge of the low cliff. From here, they could see the little town of Larmor-Baden, with its tiny harbour and its crowds of sailing boats. Vary thought of the hours of fun she and Jeff had had here, sailing Jeff's dinghy. "But you have to be very careful of the tides," she told Gil. "Look at how it's ripping through that little channel now – it's hard to make headway even with an engine." They watched a small fishing boat battle its way across the powerful stream, its engine obviously full on yet barely keeping pace with the tide. "Not so bad when it's coming in, of course," she added, "but on an outgoing tide, like now, you could get swept out of the gulf altogether."

"Not the ideal spot for a swim," Gil agreed. "But it's a marvellous view from here. Shall we stop and have our lunch?"

They settled themselves on the grassy headland and Vary produced her rolls and cheese. It didn't look much of a feast, she thought, laying them out on a cloth with a few apples, but it was surprising how good such basic food tasted, here in the open air. Maybe Thorne was right to prefer simple meals; certainly that peasant stew she'd made last night from his instructions had been every bit as delicious as the beef in wine that had caused such friction on her first night at the cottage.

She sighed, remembering Zelah's scorn over their joint cooking efforts. Alone in the kitchen, Vary and Thorne had begun to shed some of the reserve that had grown up between them since Zelah's arrival, and relax together. They could almost have achieved that precious closeness, Vary thought wistfully, if they'd only had time. But Zelah hadn't given them time. As if she sensed what was likely to happen, she came into the kitchen just when they were in the middle of chopping up a pile of vegetables, and stood there, as exotically out of place as a kingfisher in a rookery, the emerald silk of her dress clinging to her rich curves, her blue eyes mocking.

"Don't say she's got you in the kitchen, Thorne," she'd scoffed. "That's something I'd never do – I always think an apron demeans a man. Vary obviously doesn't agree."

That was one of the things Vary disliked about her – Zelah never spoke directly to her, only through Thorne. She bit her lip and said nothing, wondering if Thorne did object to helping her. But it had been his own idea.

"Since I'm not wearing an apron, the problem doesn't arise," he said imperturbably. "In any case, plenty of men are chefs, they say it's a job a woman can't do. And that's what I am today – head chef, with Vary as *my* assistant. Not the other way round."

Zelah frowned, momentarily at a loss, then shrugged. "Well, whatever turns you on," she said coolly, turning to leave the kitchen. "But I hope you aren't going to become too domesticated, Thorne darling. There's quite a lot more to life than that, remember?"

"I'm not likely to forget," Thorne replied, and Zelah disappeared, leaving a waft of expensive perfume to combat the earthier smell of onions and turnips.

Thorne caught Vary's glance and smiled. "Each to his own," he'd said. "Zelah's brilliant at her job, and quite a lady in many other ways. But as far as she's concerned, food is to be eaten, what happens to get it to the table just isn't her concern."

Vary began to chop an onion, holding her breath to try to prevent the fumes reaching her eyes. "She's lucky to be able to take that attitude. Most of us have to cook whether we like it or not."

"Oh, I agree." Thorne picked up a large piece of hard cheese and started to grate it. "Zelah *is* lucky. Her father owns a multi-million pound chemical company, the family lives in luxury and Zelah need never lift a finger if she doesn't want to. It says something for her that she trained to become a chemist – no doubt being her father's daughter helped, but she still had to work at it. But she's certainly never known what it is to be deprived."

"And you think that's lucky?" Holding her breath hadn't done any good, her eyes were beginning to smart already. "I don't. I wouldn't be like Zelah for all the millions her father might have. Living the high life – never seeing reality. Never knowing what it is to save up for something you want, the delight of finally getting it. Never *having* to work – what sort of achievement is there in that?" She paused to wipe eyes that had now begun to stream. "I'd rather be out here, making this meal with you, onion-eyes and all, than just sitting waiting for the meal to appear on the table. I'm like you, I suppose – I like to *earn* my food."

"Zelah's earned hers," he said mildly. "She's been working quite hard all day." Then his glance softened. "But I know what you mean. And I like your expression 'onion-eyes'. Except that it's just not true." He put down his knife and came over to her, holding her lightly by the shoulders. "Your eyes aren't oniony at all," he said, studying them intently with his own deep blue gaze. "They're like autumn leaves, did you know that? Autumn in an English forest – a beech forest, with the sun dappling down through the branches to a russet floor. That's what your eyes remind me of."

Vary stared up at him, her breath drying in her throat. All her nerves seemed concentrated on that light touch on her shoulders. Hypnotised, she swayed towards him, lips parted, and then Thorne turned her away from him and released her.

"Back to the chopping-board," he said lightly, and the moment was gone.

It hadn't returned again, she thought now, watching the fishing boat escape at last from the tidal rip and make good speed towards the harbour. For the rest of the evening, Thorne had retreated behind his mask, his expression inscrutable, dark eyes veiled. Zelah herself hadn't seemed able to draw him out, and in the end she'd shrugged and nestled close to him on the settee, joining him in his silence so that Vary felt herself more excluded than ever.

She was like that fishing boat, she thought sadly, caught in a current so powerful that there was no escape from it, struggle as she might.

It became a routine in the next two or three days for Vary to collect enough bread and cheese for two and disappear for the day. She never mentioned to Thorne and Zelah that she was going out with Gil; they were obviously so immersed in their work – or whatever – that they barely noticed she was gone. She assumed they thought she was either on the beach or going for long, lonely walks.

Any scruples she might have had about her friendship with Gil had long disappeared. He was good company, undemanding, friendly and he made her laugh. He clearly admired her, yet so far he hadn't made a pass of any kind. He was, she thought affectionately, rather shy, and young for his age.

"Let's go to Carnac," he exclaimed on the second morning, and off they went in the small car he had hired for the week, to roam about amongst the huge stones of the *Alignements*, wondering at their massive size and mysterious purpose. The next day it was, "Let's go to Belle-Ile" and they drove to Quiberon and took the ferry to Le Palais, main town of the island that was the French equivalent of Jersey or Guernsey, exploring the narrow streets and later driving through the small, lush valleys to finish with a bathe from one of the many secluded beaches.

"That was lovely," Vary observed as they came back on the ferry, windblown and burnished with the sun. "I'd like to spend longer there. It's a beautiful little island, just as its name says, and there's so much to see."

"Well, why don't we?" Gil said at once. "There's nothing to stop us, is there? We could go over for a few days – your Thorne won't even notice, and my friends don't look like coming yet."

Vary felt herself colour. "I don't know. It's a lovely idea, but I don't think I could. My cousin Jeff – I'm not sure when he's coming and I wouldn't like to be away—"

"Yes, you told me he'd been ill." Gil watched her face. "Well, couldn't you ring him and find out when he's coming? Then we could go."

"Yes, I could." Vary looked at him, wondering why she was so doubtful. His hazel eyes revealed nothing but friendliness. Why shouldn't she go away with him for a few days? "I'll think about it," she said temporising, and he nodded.

"No need to rush," he said lightly. "And anyway, there's a festival I want to take you to tomorrow. At a place called Guerande. They decorate the whole town with broom and it's supposed to be quite a sight. And there's a pageant, too. Should be fun."

"Mm, I'd like that." Vary felt a sense of relief that he hadn't pursued the matter of their going away. Maybe he'd forget it. There was plenty to do and see on the mainland, after all. "I've heard of the festival but I've never been here at the right time before," she went on. "I'd love to see it."

"That's a date, then." Gil slipped an arm casually round her shoulders. "It's fun being with you, Vary. I'm glad we met." And, as she turned to smile back at him, he kissed the tip of her nose.

It was bright and sunny again the next morning as Vary crept out of bed and padded through to the kitchen. Still feeling slightly guilty – though heaven knew why she should – about her friendship with Gil, she'd intended making do with a quick mug of coffee for breakfast and then slipping away without waking the others. In any case, she always tried to be out of the living room before they woke; she still wasn't sure whether or not they shared the big bedroom, and it was something she preferred not to know. She could well do without Zelah's raised eyebrows at the sight of Vary wrapped in blankets on the settee.

But to her surprise she found that this morning Thorne had beaten her to it. He was sitting on a stool, drinking coffee and reading a French newspaper. His eyes glinted when he saw her.

"Ah, the early bird in person. You've been very elusive lately, Vary. I'd begun to think you didn't live here any more."

Taken aback, and feeling at a decided disadvantage in her skimpy nightdress, Vary went across to the stove. The kettle was still hot and she spooned instant coffee into a mug and poured hot water onto it. She glanced over her shoulder at Thorne. He had evidently already been swimming, his hair was still damp, curling around his forehead to make him look more than ever like a Greek god. The hairs on his chest were damp too, tight little fists against his deep tan.

"You haven't exactly gone out of your way to entertain me," she muttered, and his brows arched still higher.

"Entertain you? Did you really expect me to?"

"No – that was a stupid thing to say. But you seem to forget I'm a free agent, I don't have to account to you for my time."

"Have I asked you to?"

"Not in so many words – yet."

Vary sat opposite him. She felt more like taking her coffee back to the living room and getting dressed as swiftly as possible, but she sensed that Thorne was out to needle her this morning and she refused to give him the satisfaction of knowing he'd succeeded. As calmly as she could, she lifted her eyes and regarded him over the rim of her pottery mug.

"So, you've been enjoying your holiday." His tone was lazy, but his eyes were like a hawk's as he watched her. Vary shrugged as noncommittally as she could manage.

"Yes, reasonably. I've been doing as you said – seeing the sights, swimming, sunbathing – generally relaxing."

"Better than spending a day cooped up in a tiny room with me, typing," he suggested.

"I didn't say that. But yes, since you put it that way – much better." His needling was getting through to her. She didn't know what this inquisition was about, but if Thorne thought she was just mooning about waiting for him to notice her again, he could think again. Irritation began to turn to a slow-burning anger.

"Not that it should matter to you," she added. "After all, I'm only waiting here for Jeff. And now you've got Zelah to help you, you'd rather I was out of the way altogether."

"Much rather," he agreed, and his eyes were blank with hostility. Vary felt a sudden ache in her throat.

They'd been getting along so well! Even after Zelah had arrived, there had still been a certain rapport between them, as on the evening when they'd made the stew together. Now, it seemed, they were back to square one.

"But of course," Thorne went on, "I quite understand that you feel you should wait for your cousin. After all, he's rather special to you, isn't he."

"Yes, he's very special." Vary finished her coffee. "Look, I'm going out for the day and we – I – want to make an early start. So if you'll excuse me . . ."

"But of course." Thorne rose to his feet and made her a mock bow. "Far be it from me to stand in the way of your social life." His eyes narrowed as she went to the door. "Did you say 'we'?"

"A friend of mine," Vary said shortly. "I *have* been here quite a few times, you know." She turned abruptly into the living room. Why had she said that? It was very nearly a lie, implying that she was going out with someone local, someone she'd known for years. Yet what harm would it have done to tell Thorne the truth about Gil? Why should it matter whether he knew or not?

Vary found this question almost impossible to answer rationally. She just knew, as surely as if he'd said so, that Thorne would have disapproved of her going around with a young man she'd known for only a few days. And, ridiculous as that might be, she didn't feel able to face his disapproval. Not just yet.

When Jeff comes, she thought, I'll bring Gil here

and introduce him. It won't matter what Thorne thinks then.

Quickly, she slipped into a cotton skirt with pale yellow and grey checks, topping it with a white sleeveless blouse with a low-cut scalloped neckline. Her tan showed a rich gold against the white, and she brushed her deep brown hair out to lie loose around her shoulders, like a shawl of russet silk. She had lost weight since coming to the cottage – all those plain meals, she thought wryly – and she clipped a grey leather belt around her narrow waist, fastening it to its last hole.

"Where is it you're going today?" Thorne asked, appearing suddenly in the doorway, and she jumped and glowered at him.

"This does happen to be the only place where I can get dressed!" she snapped. "And what does it matter to you where I'm going?"

He shrugged. "It doesn't matter at all. Only Zelah and I were thinking of taking a day off, since it's Sunday. I thought we might make a foursome of it. Or whatever it might be." He was pumping her, she thought, trying to find out how many people she was going with. Well, he was going to be disappointed.

"No, I don't think that would be a good idea," she said carelessly, slipping her feet into low-heeled sandals. "Anyway, I promised to be ready early, and Zelah isn't even up yet. You have a nice day together." She flashed him a brilliant smile from the doorway. "Bye!"

Running down the track, Vary felt absurdly pleased

with herself for her part in the little encounter. Thorne had been trying to find out who she was going out with, and he hadn't succeeded. She felt almost like a teenager, slipping out on a date forbidden by her parents. But Thorne wasn't a parent. He wasn't anything, so far as she was concerned. Just a highly arrogant man who seemed to think he had some say over what she did. And it was time he learned otherwise.

Getting to Guerande involved a drive along one of France's highways, turning off at the pretty little town of La Roche-Bernard. Here they stopped for a meal in a small restaurant in the square, finding themselves squeezed into a corner surrounded by French families enjoying their prolonged and noisy Sunday lunch. Many of them had parcels with them; daintily-wrapped boxes containing the special *gâteaux* they had bought that morning in the *pâtisserie* and would take home for family tea. Families were important to the French, Vary thought as she watched them, and so were mealtimes. A sudden pang shot through her, a wistfulness for her own family, wiped out with such abrupt brutality when she was still little more than a child. For no reason at all, she found herself wondering about Thorne's family. He had never mentioned any relations at all. Was he alone in the world? Was that the bond between them?

They left La Roche-Bernard and found the road for Guerande, crossing the edge of the Briere Natural Park as they did so. Vary gazed out of the window, fascinated. She had never been to this part before and was intrigued by the difference in the landscape.

"It's more like the English Fens," she exclaimed, as she stared at the swamps that stretched away from the road, criss-crossed by narrow channels. "So flat, and such a huge, wide sky. Oh, and now it's different again." They were now crossing a vast marsh, cut into squares like a giant chessboard, with the water lapping at their edges. At high tide, she guessed, the water must fill them. But what were these big, shallow squares for?

"Salt, isn't it?" Gil said. "The sea water washes up through all the pans and then evaporates, leaving the salt behind. They collect it all through the summer."

"Yes, of course. I've heard of it – I'd just forgotten." Vary turned from her fascinated inspection and looked at Gil in some surprise. "I thought you didn't know anything about this area?"

He shrugged. "Oh, that's just one of the things I picked up somewhere," he said lightly. "My mind's a ragbag, hadn't you noticed? Full of bits and pieces of useless knowledge."

Vary nodded and looked out of the window again. "Well, it's lucky you knew about this festival. I've never been here before and it looks lovely. Those ramparts must be nearly perfect."

Gil parked the car and they wandered along beside the walls. As Vary had said, they were in perfect condition, smooth and strong, with a green moat flowing gently at their feet. Presently, they arrived at a gateway, a miniature fort built into the wall, and went through into the narrow, bustling streets of the little town.

Vary stopped in delight. "Oh, it's pretty!" She stared

enraptured at the ancient houses, all higgledy-piggledy along the road, each one decorated with sprays of yellow broom. Gil smiled and caught her hand as she pointed, his fingers cool around her own. They explored excitedly, like two children on an outing, diving down little alleyways, meandering through the broad main street, stopping to look into the little shops that were almost all open, selling souvenirs, cakes, sweets and *crêpes*. An old woman in Breton costume sat at a stall on the pavement, selling toys; another smiled and beckoned them from behind a table laden with fruit. And everywhere there was the broom – tied over doorways, festooned around windows, strewn along the pavements.

The pageant, they discovered, was taking part in a square near the ramparts; they bought tickets and went through the high canvas screen to climb up on the walls for the best view. What it was all about, Vary never discovered: it seemed to be an amalgam of every fairy tale she had ever heard, from St George and the Dragon to Robin Hood. There was certainly a monster, which was killed by a hero riding a huge black horse, and there were certainly a troop of riders clad in medieval costume. But although much of it passed her by, it didn't matter – the colour and excitement caught at her heart and she cheered as heartily as anyone else in the crowd, and was just as sorry when it came to an end.

"That was wonderful," she told Gil as they made their way down through the chattering throng to look for something to eat and drink. "I wouldn't have missed it for anything. I'm so glad you brought me. I – oh!"

"What is it? Are you all right?" Gil stopped and looked at her in concern. "Vary, you've gone as white as a ghost."

"It's all right." Vary pulled herself together, but she couldn't tear her eyes away from the two people who were even now walking inexorably towards her. "It's just – that man there. It's Thorne – the man who's staying in the cottage. And the woman with him is Zelah Tobitt."

Gil gave them one swift glance. Before Vary could protest, he had gripped her wrist and jerked her sideways, into a narrow alley. She blinked in the darkness, wanting to protest, it didn't matter if they met Thorne, after all, it was just that it had been such a surprise seeing him . . . But Gil didn't seem to hear her explanations. Pulling her along almost roughly, he led her through the alley and into a tiny courtyard; then, with only the briefest of apologies to the family who were having tea there, he ran straight through the house that was their only way out, emerging from the front door and into another street before anyone could do more than rise to their feet.

"*Gil!*" Vary gasped, horrified. "You can't do that! Charge through people's houses! I told you, it wouldn't *matter*, meeting Thorne. He doesn't have any say over what I do. Gil, listen—"

But Gil didn't pause until they were back outside the ramparts and making for the car. There, he pulled the door open and thrust Vary inside. And it wasn't until he was inside too, winding down the windows to let out the heat, that he faced her and relaxed.

"Sorry about that," he said. "I know you said it didn't matter, but you obviously didn't want to meet him. And neither did I – he looks just the kind of jumped up, arrogant know-all I prefer to avoid. Vary—" his voice grew suddenly intense "—is it true that he's nothing to you? Are you really sure?"

"Of course I'm sure," she answered, fighting down a sudden surge of longing to be with Thorne in the streets of Guerande, exclaiming over the broom and laughing at the pageant with him. Walking hand in hand with him . . . "Of course I'm sure," she repeated. "I'm only sharing the cottage with him because of a misunderstanding over the dates. And because I've got to wait for Jeff. After this, I don't suppose I'll ever see or hear from Thorne again." She tried fruitlessly to ignore the stab of pain her own words gave her, and pushed away from her mind the vision they brought of a long, lonely future.

"In that case—" Gil drew a deep breath "—I hadn't meant to say this to you yet, Vary. But these past few days – well, you've become very important to me. I know you won't feel the same way, but I've got to tell you, anyway." He took her hands and Vary looked quickly at him, suddenly afraid of what he might be about to say. "Vary, I think I'm falling in love with you. Is there – do you think there's any chance at all you could feel the same way for me?" He shook her hands slightly, his urgency communicating itself through their clasped fingers. "If you can't say yes, Vary, please don't say no – not until you've given me a chance."

Vary stared blindly at him. Love? How could he talk about love? Love was what she felt for Thorne. Love was pain, a constant, gnawing torment that could only be eased by reciprocation. It was a kind of personal hell that one carried around, a hell from which there was no escape.

Could Gil possibly feel that agony for her? He seemed so careless, so light-hearted. And yet – if he did indeed feel it, that left her with a heavy responsibility. She couldn't be the cause of anyone suffering the pain she suffered whenever she thought of Thorne and the bleak future she must spend without him.

"Don't say no, Vary," Gil begged her. "I'm sorry if I've blurted it all out too soon. Let's just go on as we have been – enjoying ourselves together. Maybe it'll come – I *know* it'll come."

Vary looked at him sadly. She knew that it wouldn't, not while Thorne remained on the same earth. But she couldn't tell Gil that, couldn't see the pain flood his eyes. Somehow, she would have to make him realise gradually that she could never love him. She would be kinder to him than Thorne had been to her.

But then, Thorne didn't know she loved him, did he? All he knew was that she'd been willing to go to bed with him. And to him, that was clearly something quite different.

Chapter Ten

"And just where," Thorne demanded silkily, "have you been until this hour?"

Vary stopped in the doorway and blinked at him. He had evidently been waiting up for her; he was wearing a towelling robe in deep blue that accentuated the brilliance of his eyes. Eyes which she saw were at this moment smouldering with anger.

Vary's own temper began to rise at once. "Just what's that to do with you?" she retorted. "Where I go, what I do and what time I come back is my business. And now that I am back, I'd like to go to bed. So if you don't mind—"

Thorne didn't move. He stayed where he was, filling the centre of the small room, the low light casting his shadow like a looming giant on the wall behind him. His brows drew together in a scowl, and Vary shrank away from him in spite of herself. Fleetingly, she wondered where Zelah was.

"I happen to feel responsible for you," he rasped. "Your cousin isn't here to keep an eye on you and I—"

"Oh, for heaven's sake!" Exasperation burst out of her. "Look, I'm touring Europe *alone*, remember? I look after myself. Jeff doesn't 'keep an eye' on me – nobody does. Least of all you. And now, if you don't mind, I'd like to go to bed!"

"When you've told me where you've been and why you're so late." He evidently had no intention at all of moving, and Vary sighed.

"Do I have to repeat that it's none of your business?" she enquired. "I've been out with a friend, as I told you this morning. We had dinner together, and he's just brought me home. That's all you need to know, so—"

Thorne pounced. "So you've been out with a man!"

"Yes, I have, and what of it? I'm a grown woman, you know. I've been on dates with men before."

"I don't doubt it," he said slowly, his burning eyes fixed on her face. "And with what results, I wonder?"

"I beg your pardon?" Vary's tone was icy.

"Just how liberated a lady are you, Vary?" he went on insinuatingly. "When you first came here, all wide-eyed innocence, I didn't believe in it – thought it was just a ploy. Then I found you really were who you said you were, and I thought again. Maybe there were still a few untouched women in the world. It was a new idea, a refreshing change. I treated you with respect – or maybe you didn't notice. But now . . ." he glanced at his watch, "I just wonder whether I wasn't right to start with. You've been out since early this morning and it's now midnight. You admit you've been with a man, but

159

you won't tell me who he is. It all adds up to a guilty conscience."

To her annoyance, Vary felt her face flush scarlet. Thankful for the dim light, though uncomfortably sure that Thorne's hawklike gaze wouldn't miss even the slightest change in her expression, she turned her head away. Her heart was thumping with fury. Just who did he think he was? How *dare* he question her like this?

"My conscience isn't in the least guilty," she answered tightly. "You wouldn't expect it to be, would you – not if I were the kind of girl you seem to think I am. But as it happens, I'm not. Why you should be so interested, I can't imagine, but since you are, you might as well know that you were right second time. I haven't had any serious boyfriends and I haven't slept with anyone. Not before I came here, nor since." Her flush deepened as she recalled belatedly that she'd been all too willing to sleep with Thorne. "And as for your treating me with respect," she went on scathingly, "no, I didn't notice. I simply thought that you were too immersed in your work to see me as a woman at all. Or that maybe you weren't the kind of man to be interested."

She stopped, wondering if she'd gone too far, and then took a step back as Thorne came towards her. But there was nowhere to step back to, and she came to a halt, her back against the closed door, as Thorne moved ominously closer.

"Oh, I'm the kind of man to be interested all right," he said softly, and reached out to lay one hand on her shoulder. His thumb moved gently on her neck, and Vary shivered with a mixture of fear and sudden uncontrollable desire. "I thought I'd proved that to you on the night Zelah arrived. But of course, we weren't able to take things to their logical conclusion then, were we? Maybe we should do that now. It might clear the air."

Vary pressed her trembling body against the door, looking up at him with eyes like deep forest pools. Inwardly, she cursed her body, knowing that it threatened to betray her yet again. What *was* it about Thorne that had this disastrous effect on her? Why did she feel this scorching need to be in his arms? Why did she have to love him?

"Don't come any nearer," she said in a low voice. "Don't touch me." Perhaps he would think that she was revolted by him. Perhaps he wouldn't realise that, to her, the slightest touch could mean total submission.

But Thorne's gently moving thumb pressed a fraction harder, drawing her unwillingly closer. Surely, she thought, he must hear the thunder of her heart; surely he must feel the heat of the blood that surged through her veins. There was a slight, cruel smile on his face, and she knew that he could sense each tremor of her body and correctly assess its cause. He knows very well how he affects me, she thought in dizzying dismay, and he's going to take complete advantage of it.

"Leave me alone, Thorne, I beg you," she breathed, but her lips were still parted from the words when he bent his head and laid a kiss upon them. It was a gentle kiss, almost tender, but with her first quick gasp it deepened to an assault, an invasion that plundered the sweetness of her mouth, sending waves of desire pulsing through her entire body so that she moaned and clung to him. She felt a grunt of satisfaction deep in his chest, and her whirling emotions eddied like billowing waves, as unstoppable as the incoming tide, as they washed away all her doubts and fears, drawing her into a current of overpowering need that had at all costs to be satisfied.

"Vary," he muttered against her hair, "Vary, my love, don't you know what you're doing to me? Don't you realise what's happening? Why are you so cruel, so uncaring, so—"

Vary broke away from him. "Cruel? Uncaring? *Me?* Thorne, you've got it all wrong! *You're* the one who's cruel – you've made it so plain you hate me, you can't wait to be rid of me." She shook her head, bewildered. "And yet you want to know what I'm doing: where I've been and who with. I don't understand, Thorne. Just what *do* you feel for me? Is it just desire, or is it more?" She held back from his seeking lips, her eyes on his, searching for the truth. "Or do you just have to make a conquest of every woman you meet? Is *that* the sort of man you are?" She glanced at the bedroom door, securely closed. "What about Zelah? Does she know you're out here, trying to make love to me? Will you go back to her when you've had everything you want from me? Doesn't she know what kind of man you are – or doesn't she care?"

Thorne's hands stilled on her body. For a long

moment, he regarded her. The fire had died from his eyes, leaving them cold and empty. Vary watched him, feeling a disturbing conflict of emotion. She hated herself for the things she had just said, wanted to unsay them so that he would continue to love her, to give her what she so desperately wanted. And at the same time, she was relieved. This wasn't the right way, a voice inside told her. It had to be different from this for her and Thorne. If it were ever to happen at all.

"All right," Thorne said bleakly, "let's stop playing, Vary." Was that all it was? *Playing*? Her blood simmered. "Let's have the truth." The dark eyes, sombre as a starless sky, raked her body. "I know exactly where you've been today. I saw you there – in Guerande. I saw you, with this man, whoever he is. And you saw me. Didn't you? Didn't you?"

The force of his burning glance was like a blow. Vary gasped and rocked a little. So their wild dash through the alleys had been in vain. Thorne had seen them, and probably Zelah had too. Vary closed her eyes, imagining the older woman's glee as she watched their panic-stricken flight.

"Well?" he pressed her. "Didn't you see me? Isn't that why you ran away? Because you were afraid to meet me? Because you were ashamed to introduce me to this – this pick-up of yours?"

"No, it wasn't like that at all," Vary began wildly, but another searing glance brought her to floundering silence. Because if it hadn't been like that, she just didn't know how to explain it. She hadn't wanted to meet Thorne and Zelah. She hadn't wanted to introduce them to Gil.

The memory of Gil's words to her in the car – the way he'd talked later on, the almost desperate pleas he'd made for her understanding, for her love, it all came flooding back. She lifted her chin and faced Thorne defiantly. There couldn't be any two men more different, she realised with a blinding flash of insight. Gil was everything Thorne was not – kind, gentle, caring, fun to be with. "It's not what you think at all," she told him steadily. "Gil is the nicest man I've ever met. And he happens to like me a lot too. In fact—" she swallowed "—he's asked me to marry him."

"To *marry* him?"

The words echoed oddly in the quiet room. Vary wondered if Zelah were really asleep in that other room, or whether she were awake and listening avidly to all this. She risked another glance at Thorne and saw that something seemed to have drained the colour from his face. He was looking oddly shocked. But then, so he might since he had until today believed her to be spending her time entirely alone.

"That's ridiculous," he said harshly, and Vary felt another spurt of anger, even though she'd used almost the same words to Gil himself not much more than an hour ago. She closed her eyes momentarily. She had intended to come quietly into the cottage and think – think about everything that had happened, about the hopelessness of her feelings for Thorne, about whether there might indeed be a future for her with Gil. She'd reckoned without Thorne waiting up for her.

"What's so ridiculous about it?" she demanded, opening her eyes again to find Thorne still watching her, the hollows of his face shadowed and gaunt in the lamplight. "At least he's made me an honourable proposal, which is more than you've ever done. At least he's asked me to marry him. At least he hasn't tried to make love to me, against my will."

Thorne gave a hollow laugh. "Against your will! Now, that's really funny. I haven't noticed you resisting much when I've touched you – you practically burst into flames every time." He reached out to Vary's scarlet cheeks and ran his finger lightly down her face, tracing down the side of her neck and into the cleft of her breasts. "I could take you now and you wouldn't lift a finger to stop me," he said contemptuously, his fingertips slipping inside her blouse to caress the swelling curve beneath. "Are you going to tell me it's just with me, or do you come to the boil like this with every man who lays hands on you?"

Furiously, Vary twisted away. "You're disgusting! I told you not to touch me. Now, *leave me alone.* I've told you, I've just agreed to marry another man, or does that mean nothing to you?"

"Not when you react to me like you did a few minutes ago." He watched her narrowly. "Is that true, Vary? That you've agreed to marry him? Or are you just saying it to taunt me?"

Vary hesitated. She didn't want to admit it wasn't

165

true, that she hadn't given Gil an answer. But neither did she want Thorne to think that she had come into his arms, hungry for his touch, direct from a promise to marry another man. She shrugged. "I told him I'd think about it," she muttered, and Thorne nodded.

"And presumably you already have. I'm simply going on the way you responded just now," he added silkily, and Vary's temper boiled over.

"All right," she snapped. "So I *do* respond to you. That means nothing, *nothing*, do you hear?" It cut her to the soul to deny the love she had for him, but she took a deep breath and continued, "And now that you know the true situation, I hope you'll have the courtesy to leave me alone – as I've already asked. Don't touch me again, all right? I may respond on one level, but on all the levels that really matter, I'm disgusted and appalled by my own reactions. If you touch me again, I shall leave the cottage – and you can explain to Jeff just why I couldn't wait. No doubt you'll be able to think of something convincing, but don't forget, I'll have an opportunity to tell him the truth some other time. And I shall – make no mistake about that!"

Thorne turned away. There was no way of gauging his reaction and Vary wanted to fling her arms around him, to beg his forgiveness, to tell him she loved him, deeply, truly, and always would. But she held back. That wasn't what he wanted to hear. He didn't want to hear anything at all about her feelings. All he'd wanted was to satisfy himself with her body. He was simply sulking, like a spoilt child who had been refused yet another sweet.

It wasn't enough. Not for Vary.

"And now, if you don't mind," she said, keeping a rigid control on her voice, "I really would like to go to bed."

Without a word, Thorne crossed to the door of the small bedroom. Without looking at her, he opened it and went inside. The living room seemed suddenly bleak and empty without him.

Vary stood quite still, swallowing back the tears. She sank down on the settee, still looking at the door. Perhaps a miracle would happen; perhaps Thorne would come out again, cross the room to take her in his arms, love her with the tenderness, the feeling, the sincerity for which she yearned.

But no miracle happened. Although Vary sat quite still, watching it, for over half an hour, the door remained closed. And she was forced in the end to slip out of her clothes and huddle into the blankets on the settee, where she lay for the rest of the night, her body a smouldering furnace of frustration, her mind wandering a confused path between waking and disturbed, unhappy dreams.

"Well, well, well. So the sleeper awakes." Zelah's meticulously shaped eyebrows rose as Vary came out into the garden. "We didn't expect to see you for quite a while, after your exciting day out. Thorne's just gone to the village for croissants. So we've time for a little chat." Her blue eyes had lost their baby look this morning and were hard, as sharp as the points of needles. "We don't seem to have had much time for talking, do we, what with one thing and another?"

Vary said nothing. She helped herself to coffee and debated whether to stay. But it would have been childish and ostentatious to walk away. She sat down, sipping the coffee, grateful for its heat and strength.

"I hear you've got yourself engaged," Zelah went on, her mouth smiling. "Congratulations."

"Well, not exactly," Vary said guardedly. "I haven't given him an answer yet."

"But you will, won't you? I mean, you may not get too many chances." Vary's head snapped up, but Zelah's face was as smooth and bland as butter. "There don't seem to be that many personable young men about these days. Not that I have to worry, of course – not with Thorne continually begging me to marry him."

Something heavy sank in Vary's stomach. "Does he?" she asked, the words dragging out of her. "Beg you to marry him?"

"Oh, my dear!" Zelah's laugh was more like a purr. "He never stops. Of course, I will in the end – and he knows it, really – but it does no harm at all to keep that little bit of uncertainty in a man's mind. Keeps him on his toes. Of course, you know this, it's what you're doing with your young man, isn't it? We have to look after ourselves, don't we? There's no fun in being taken for granted." She gave Vary an 'all girls together' look. Vary didn't respond, and after a moment or two the blonde tossed back her glossy hair and continued,

"I must admit, I was just a touch worried about you and Thorne. That night when I arrived – well, I know I behaved *very* badly—" again, the conspiratorial look "—but I really did think you were just a village tart that he'd brought back for his own amusement. And then when he took off after you and followed you to the beach, and didn't come back for simply *ages* – well, I did begin to wonder. Not that I was *really* worried, of course – I've known Thorne too long for that. He's a man, after all, and any man needs a certain amount of female company, don't you agree? And he always does come back to me after these little forays from the straight and narrow. But that night, well, he did seem a little more upset than I expected, and I did worry, just a little." She gave Vary her most charming smile. "I realised there was nothing at all to worry about, naturally, as soon as I saw you next morning."

"Did you?" Vary's voice was tight and she couldn't summon up an answering smile as she recalled that morning and the contrast she must have made, in her old shirt and shorts, with Zelah's glossy perfection.

"Oh, yes. You're not Thorne's type at all – not really." Zelah smoothed her pale green linen skirt with a complacent hand. "No, he does tend to go for sophistication, in spite of all his talk about the Third World. The simple peasant style might have intrigued him for a while, but it could never have lasted. No, I'd say you were really quite fortunate that I came along that evening. You might have got quite badly hurt otherwise, and I wouldn't want that."

169

That was exactly what Vary had thought, but she wasn't going to say so. Instead, she muttered something about being surprised that Thorne should go for glamour when his working life was spent so close to squalor.

"But that's just why!" Zelah exclaimed. "He isn't really cut out for that life at all. He loves everything to do with money – and he's got plenty of it himself, did you realise that? Oh, yes. His family are quite wealthy. His father's a surgeon, and his mother's an interior designer. And they both have money of their own. Thorne's work is just a rebellion against all that, but it won't last. Take it from me, once he's finished this research into the new drug he'll be very glad to come back to civilisation. With all the publicity over the drug, as well as his TV series and books, he'll find plenty of doors open to him. And then, of course, we can get married."

Vary stared at her. She remembered the quiet intensity of Thorne's voice as he told her that his work was his life. Could Zelah be right? Would he really turn his back on the valuable work he was doing and embrace the fleshpots of financial success? She felt slightly sick at the thought.

"But none of this need worry you," Zelah went on cheerfully. "Once your cousin arrives and you can see how he is, you'll be free to go on. Will you continue with your sightseeing trip, do you think? Or will you marry this boy – what *is* his name, by the way? – and forget Europe?"

"I don't know yet. I haven't decided." Vary heard the

sounds of Thorne approaching along the path. "Look –
I don't really want any breakfast. I'll just slip down to
the beach. I – I'll probably be out all day."

"Of course." Zelah gave her a smile that reminded
her forcibly of that of a shark, about to swallow its
prey. "You run along and enjoy yourself. I know just
what it's like to be in love – other people simply don't
matter, do they?"

Don't they? Vary thought as she collected her bag
and ran through the bushes just before Thorne came into
view. Perhaps that's how I know I'm not in love – with
Gil, anyway. Because Thorne matters far too much.

Gil wasn't on the beach yet, and Vary sat down on a
rock, staring sombrely at the sea. Her mind was crowded
with a bewilderment of ideas and emotions, and she was
thankful to have time to sort them out.

Since she had arrived home last night to be inter-
cepted by Thorne, she hadn't even had time to decide
what to do about Gil's proposal. It had come as a
shock – that sudden declaration in the car, after their
hasty flight from Thorne and Zelah. Vary had been
too taken aback to give him any answer at all, other
than to stutter out her surprise. And later, as they'd sat
together over a candlelit dinner, she'd listened bemused
to Gil's plans.

"We could do Europe together," he'd urged, his hazel
eyes alight. "It'd be much more fun than going round
on our own, separately. We could get married here,
before we start. I don't know what the formalities are

but it must be possible, or we could wait until we go back to England, whichever you'd rather. But I think you'd rather be married, wouldn't you? And I know I would."

"But – but I've never even thought of you in that way." She was immediately afraid that she'd hurt him, and went on quickly, "Gil, I've only known you a few days – it's too soon to know whether we could – could love each other." It hadn't been to soon to know about Thorne, she thought at once, and pushed the thought away. There was no future with Thorne. Did that have to mean there was no future at all?

"It's not too soon." Gil's eyes were warm. "I knew as soon as I saw you. And I think you know too, whatever you say." His hands cradled hers. "Vary – maybe you're right to be cautious. But there *is* something between us, isn't there? Something more than mere friendship?"

Vary looked at him. His eyes reminded her of those of an imploring spaniel, and she felt the same reluctance to refuse him what he wanted. A walk – a lifetime. What did it really matter, when Thorne was never going to want her in the way that this man did?

"Don't let's rush into anything, Gil," she said gently. "It really is too quick for me. Let's just go on enjoying ourselves, and see what happens. Can we?"

"We can do anything you want," he told her, and his fingers tightened over hers. "It's for you to say, Vary. I won't rush you – all I ask is that you don't keep me waiting for *too* long. Is that a bargain?"

"Yes," she said simply, and her eyes misted with

tears. Why did everything have to be so complicated? "That's a bargain, Gil."

And she had honestly intended to think seriously about his proposal once she'd got back to the cottage. Thorne had effectively driven all her good intentions out of her mind. But now there was time.

Thoughtfully, Vary watched the smooth surface of the bay. The usual fishing boats were chugging across to the port, and there was a little desultory activity around the harbour walls. Nobody ever seemed to hurry in this quiet place, yet there must be other human dramas going on in those peaceful-looking cottages. She sighed for all those who were struggling through the maze of life without a guide, and wondered if anyone ever learned all the answers. And by the time they had, did they need them any more? Or did life go on being difficult into old age?

Suppose she married Gil. What would her life be like then? He'd tried to tell her, last night in that little restaurant with the mouthwatering smells of French cooking wafting from the kitchen. He'd told her of his plans for their trip round Europe together, having fun just as they'd had fun during the past few days. He'd told her how, when they eventually returned to England, he would find a job and they'd buy a little house and live in it together, bringing up their family. It sounded peaceful, almost idyllic, as he described it. And not so long ago it would have been just what Vary wanted.

But now – why did she have to keep thinking of heat,

flies, dust and disease? Why did her blood stir at the thought of combating these things, helping those who were trapped by their environment? Why did a life lived amid squalor, working all the hours there were, having to cope with despair and disappointment as well as the occasional reward of seeing a child grow up whole instead of maimed and deformed, seem so much more exciting?

If she suggested to Gil that they might together join some organisation that would send them to these places to help, what would he say? Would he be horrified, or would he agree? Was she even sure that that was what she wanted to do?

A shout interrupted her thoughts, and Vary glanced around. Gil was coming towards her along the beach, his fair hair ruffled by the breeze, his face alight with pleasure at seeing her.

If she told him there could never be a future for them together, would he feel the same despair as she felt concerning Thorne? Could she inflict that on him, on anyone? And was there any need to do so?

Once again she thought, if there's nothing for me with Thorne, does it mean there's nothing with anyone? Mightn't there be some happiness with Gil? Couldn't I simply live the way he wants: have fun, settle down into suburban domesticity?

She stood up, smiling and waving as he hurried across the beach. I won't say anything today, she thought. We'll just do as I said last night – keep things the way they are, for a little while longer.

It wasn't in the least likely that things would change between her and Thorne. Zelah would see to that. But, just for a little while, she had to go on hoping. She needed that hope.

It seemed to be all she had.

Chapter Eleven

"Lot of fuss about nothing," Jeff said blithely over the phone. "I was just a waste of a bed in that hospital. If they'd left me at home I'd have got over it by myself in half the time."

"I think you must be the only man I know who isn't a hypochondriac," Vary said, relieved to hear him sounding so cheerful. "All the same, it must have been serious for them to take you in. You will take care of yourself now, won't you, Jeff? I mean, no swimming in cold lakes or night climbing on the mountains."

"Vary, it's the middle of the summer! I'm not going to catch cold now. I'm better, okay? Cured, back to full health, fit as a fiddle." He spoilt it all by coughing and she couldn't help laughing at him. "Well, all right, I do still feel a bit fragile and yes, I am taking care. I promise."

"And are you coming over soon? I'm really looking forward to seeing you. There's so much—" She stopped. What was there to tell Jeff? About Thorne – about Gil? She hardly knew herself.

"Well, you know I was hoping to come pretty soon,"

he said, and her heart sank a little at his tone. "But what with all this fuss and bother, and things I've got to sort out here, well, I'm not sure I'm going to be able to after all."

"Not at all?" Vary exclaimed in disappointment. "Not during the whole summer?"

"Well, not for a couple of weeks at least. Maybe not till the end of the holidays. And then I daresay you'll be off on the next part of your trip."

Vary had almost forgotten her trip round Europe. With all the turmoil over Thorne, the new relationship that had seemed to be forming between them until Zelah's advent, and then Gil, the idea of journeying on by herself seemed oddly unappealing. But Jeff was right. If she were to go on with it, she'd have to be thinking about it soon. Otherwise it would be autumn, and then winter would be setting in, and she really needed to be further south by then.

"But I don't want to go without seeing you," she said forlornly. "I've been looking forward to seeing you. And I felt dreadful that I wasn't there when you were ill."

"Don't be silly," her cousin said briskly. "You didn't even know. And that's not your fault either – I wouldn't let them contact you. There was nothing you could do and I didn't want to spoil your holiday . . . Look, you just enjoy yourself and I'll get sorted out here as quickly as I can and try to come sooner, all right? I want to see you too – make sure you're still in one piece!" He laughed.

Still in one piece. And am I? Vary wondered, as she replaced the receiver. Sometimes I feel as if I've been taken apart and put back together, and not very expertly either.

She closed the door of the telephone box behind her and walked along the lane. Thorne and Zelah were going out for the day and Gil would be here soon. The sun was shining and all she need do was to follow Jeff's bidding and enjoy herself.

Surely that was easy enough. So why did it seem as if there were a shadow over the sun?

"So this is your rural retreat." Gil stood at the cottage door, his bright eyes darting around the small living room. "Very nice. Very nice indeed." He took a step inside. "Can I browse? Do you mind?"

"No, of course not." Vary cast an anxious glance outside. In spite of her words, she was uneasy, afraid that Thorne and Zelah might return at any moment, even though she knew that they intended to be out all day. She shook herself angrily. What did it matter if they did come back and find her here with Gil? The cottage did, after all, belong to *her* cousin. There was no reason why she shouldn't invite whom she liked.

All the same, she knew she'd be happier when Gil had seen all he wanted to and decided to go somewhere else. And she could be quite safe in the assumption that he'd do that – Gil's concentration span, she'd noticed, never seemed to focus on one subject for very long. She'd even wondered once or twice how he'd ever managed to complete his university course.

"I'm a fun person," he'd declared when she'd teased him about this. "I can concentrate when I have to – I just don't think I have to, most of the time. Now, what shall we do this afternoon?"

Vary watched from the doorway as he prowled round the little room, picking things up to examine them, putting them down again in not quite the right place. He roamed out to the kitchen, then returned and opened Zelah's bedroom door.

"I say!" He stood gazing into the room. "She's quite a girl, your Zelah, isn't she? The place is practically drowned in Chanel – and just get a load of that negligée! It doesn't exactly go with the environment, does it?" He disappeared and returned with a froth of black lace over one arm. "Bet she looks a million dollars in this."

"She ought to," Vary replied with asperity. "It looks as if that's what it cost. Gil, do come out. You shouldn't be poking around in her room." But she still couldn't help being fascinated by the exotic creation that Gil was holding up for her inspection. She had never seen Zelah wearing it, presumably it was kept for the bedroom. For Thorne to see. She felt suddenly sick.

"Gil, put it back and come out," she begged. "Suppose they came back. Please, Gil."

"But I haven't seen everything yet. There's another door." He tried it. "It's locked. What's in there?"

"It's Thorne's workroom." By now, she was in a fever of anxiety. Showing Gil the cottage was one thing. Letting him make free with Zelah's belongings or Thorne's work was quite different. They would have every right to be angry if they came back and discovered him, and the inevitable scene was something that Vary didn't want to face. "Please, Gil, do come out."

"But why is it locked?" He came out and looked at the second door, between the bedroom and the living room. "Does that go into the same room?"

"Yes." Helplessly, Vary watched as Gil tried that too. "Gil, please don't. Thorne's very particular about his work – he doesn't like anyone interfering with it. Anyway, that door's locked too. They always lock it when they go out."

"So I see. I wonder why?" Gil's eyes were bright with curiosity. "Well, never mind, I've seen what the cottage is like. I don't suppose that room's any different from the rest." He came quickly across the room and gave Vary a light kiss. "Don't look so worried, my sweet. I shan't employ my well-known skills at breaking and entering. Why not make me a big cup of coffee, and then we'll decide where we're going next."

Vary gave him an uncertain smile and slipped through to the kitchen. There were times when she wasn't quite certain about Gil. She was beginning to think he wasn't quite the light-hearted, uncomplicated 'fun' person he claimed to be. But there really wasn't anything odd about his behaviour this morning, she chided herself. He was just being Gil – as curious as a young animal exploring new territory, but forgetting it within five minutes as his eager restlessness took him on to new discoveries. He hadn't quite grown up yet, that was all, she thought fondly as she spooned coffee into mugs. He was still very much a boy. And all the nicer for it! In any case, it was her own guilty conscience that was making her anxious this morning, and that was just plain ridiculous. There was no reason why she and Gil shouldn't stay in the cottage all day if they wanted to.

In the end, that was what they did. It was peaceful in the garden with its shaggy lawn, and they carried their coffee out into the sunshine and basked, chatting easily and laughing over nothing. Vary's anxiety eased. In a mood of defiance – who was she defying? she wondered briefly – she fetched bread and cheese and a bottle of wine. They moved into the shade of the twisted old pear tree and sat close together, drinking from the same glass, exchanging butterfly kisses. It was fun, happily lighthearted, and as romantic as a girl could wish, she thought sleepily as she settled against Gil's shoulder for a doze.

So why did it all seem so superficial?

The sun was casting longer shadows when they finally stirred, and a cool breeze ruffled across Vary's brow and woke her. For a few moments she thought she was lying close to Thorne, and a deep contentment warmed her body. She turned, still half asleep, her lips parted for a kiss, and then woke completely with a kicking heart as a darker shadow fell across her face and Thorne's deep, sardonic tones bit into her mind.

"The babes in the wood, no less," he drawled and

she blinked up at him, unhappily aware of the contrast between her dream and the reality. "What a very pretty sight to come home to."

As Gil moved, Vary sat up, brushing back her long, mahogany hair. Behind Thorne she could see Zelah, and the older woman's raised brows and amused smile brought an instant irritation. The feeling warred with mortification at having been discovered like this, and she shook Gil's arm rather more roughly than she intended.

"Wake up, Gil! It's Thorne and Zelah – they're back."

Gil scrambled to his feet. He ran his fingers through his hair, dusted his shorts and held out his hand, smiling with boyish charm. Vary stayed where she was, watching as Thorne looked the younger man up and down, then she stood up and took her place beside Gil.

"Marvellous to meet you," Gil said as easily as if they'd met at a party. "Vary's told me a lot about you. I'm Gil Mitchell. I've been seeing quite a lot of Vary lately."

"So I've gathered." Thorne's eyes were hard. "I was beginning to wonder why she didn't bring you home to meet us. Presumably you'd intended to leave before we returned."

Vary broke in. "There was no reason why I should bring Gil 'home to meet you', as you put it – you're not my parents, or responsible for me in any way. And whether we'd intended staying or going isn't any of your business."

Gil took her hand. "Don't get so upset, Vary. It doesn't matter. I'm sure Thorne didn't mean that the way it sounded." He smiled again at the older man. "So you're Thorne Moran. I never guessed I'd have the luck to meet a famous author. Your TV serial's got the nation on tenterhooks, so I've heard."

Thorne shot Vary a quick, inimical look. "You told him about that?" And just what else did you tell him? his eyes demanded.

"Oh, we've had some really interesting talks," Gil said easily. "I've been fascinated. But you won't want to hear about all that. I expect you're dying for a cup of tea. And nobody's introduced me to this beautiful woman yet."

"This is Zelah," Vary said shortly. "Zelah Tobitt. She's helping Thorne with his work." Thorne was never going to forgive her for this, she knew. And she realised suddenly just how much she had told Gil, almost without realising it. She'd never actually poured out the whole story – it had all been let slip in bits and pieces. But each particle had been carefully gathered up by Gil and stored away in his memory, and she was terrified he would reveal to Thorne just how much there was.

"Zelah." Gil shook the blonde's hand warmly, and Vary saw their eyes meet. It was an odd look – not recognition – but almost so. As if they'd recognised each other on a deeper level than having simply met before. Was it what happened when people talked about love at first sight? she wondered. But surely not – Gil was in love with her, wasn't he? And she would have laid bets that he wasn't Zelah's type.

She must have been imagining it. The look vanished, almost as quickly as it came, too rapid to be identified. Zelah was speaking in her normal cool tones, her expression once again amused and patronising.

"So you're the secret lover," she was saying. "Thorne and I have been consumed with curiosity, haven't we, darling? But it's nice to see Vary so happy. She's been positively radiant since she met you. I'm afraid she was distinctly peaky when I first arrived."

"Love cures all," Gil said lightly. "Well, isn't this fun? We ought to celebrate. What about that cup of tea, Vary my sweet? And then dinner out somewhere special, the four of us. Don't you think that's a good idea?"

"Fabulous," Thorne said ironically, "but I'm afraid you'll have to count us out. Zelah and I have some work to do. We shan't be going anywhere tonight."

"No, isn't that a shame?" Zelah gave them all a brilliant smile. "Another time. You'll be around for a few more days, won't you, Gil?"

"Oh, yes." He glanced at her and again there was that odd flash of communication. "I'm staying at the local *auberge*. Once Vary's ready to move on, we'll make our plans, but she wants to stay to see her cousin."

Vary gave him a quick look. He was implying that they'd already agreed to go on together, and she'd never said any such thing. But now wasn't the time to argue about it. And what of the friends that he had told her on that first morning that he was waiting for? Weren't they coming after all? Or had they never been coming – had it been just an excuse to spend some time with her?

"I don't think I want to go out for a meal either, Gil," she said. "I've got a bit of a headache. The sun and the wine, I expect." She felt Thorne's eyes on her and wondered if he was remembering that other time when she'd fallen asleep in the sun. "D'you mind if I don't come?"

"Not in the least," he said cheerfully. "You stay here and rest, Vary my love." He dropped a kiss on the top of her head. "I'm not all that hungry myself. Tell you what – you have an early night and we'll have a good long day out tomorrow. Suit you?" He gave them all a smile, sketched a wave with his hand and sauntered to the gate. "It's been really nice to meet you at last," he added, as he disappeared into the lane.

There was a short silence. Vary kept her eyes on the ground, not daring to risk a glance at Thorne. She didn't need to see his expression, anyway, she could feel the disapproval emanating from him like a tangible force.

"Quite an attractive young man," Zelah said at last. "I congratulate you, Vary. There's something very appealing about the baby-faced type, isn't there?"

"I've never thought about it," Vary said, her voice wooden. "I just find him pleasant company."

Thorne moved abruptly. "And that's a good enough basis for marriage? Pleasant company? You haven't given any consideration to his ability to keep you, I suppose, to support you and any family you may have? You haven't wondered what he might be like in a crisis – and we all have a crisis or two to face now and then. You haven't thought about him as a *man* at all, or only in one way!" Vary's eyes dragged themselves up to his face and she saw that his brows were drawn together in a thunderous scowl. "He's a lightweight, Vary – a nonentity. And not, unless I'm much mistaken, particularly scrupulous. Marry him, and you're asking for a lifetime of trouble. That's if you could stay with him for a lifetime – which I doubt."

"Well, that's something you don't need to worry about, isn't it!" she retorted. "What happens to me after I leave here isn't your concern. It's not something you're ever likely to know, because I shan't be sending you any postcards. And I'll make sure Jeff doesn't keep you up to date on my life, too. Once I walk out of here, Thorne Moran, I'll be walking out of your life completely and for ever, so there really isn't any point in your worrying now, is there!"

"Oh, I'm not worrying. I'm simply amazed that anyone, even you, could be such a fool. All right, he's pleasant and charming and all the rest of it, but when it comes to the crunch those aren't the important things. What's important in this life, Vary, are integrity and strength of character and purpose. I doubt if that young man has any of those qualities. I'll be very glad if I'm proved wrong."

Vary gazed at him. She knew that she agreed wholeheartedly with Thorne about what was important in life. Deep down, she suspected, they would agree about a great deal more. Her heart ached to be able to acknowledge this, to hear him say that he felt that way too, but it would never happen. Not only Gil, but Zelah, stood in their way. While she was about, her red-tipped fingers stroking Thorne's arm as they were doing now, they could never come together.

As if on cue, Zelah spoke, her voice huskily amused. "Stop teasing the child, Thorne. You're upsetting her. One should never interfere with first love, it's so sweet. Isn't that right, Vary?"

Vary turned away, unable to answer. First love – Gil wasn't her first love. Thorne was her first love, and there was nothing sweet about the savage yearning she felt for him, the raw ache that drove her to a fury of frustration and made her quarrel with him at every opportunity, as if by doing so she could destroy the incessant need, wipe out her longing. A hollow laugh rose in her throat. Nothing would do that – nothing. It was a torture she had been condemned to suffer for the rest of her life.

Zelah was still speaking. "Anyway, I must fly, I've remembered something I wanted from the village shop. Shan't be long. And listen, you two—" she shook a playful finger "—no squabbling while I've gone, understand? Let's all be friends, it's so much cosier."

Thorne watched her go, an odd expression on his face. He turned to Vary. "Did you hear that? No squabbling." There was a quirk to his chiselled lips that could have been humour.

"As if we were two children being left by their

nanny," Vary muttered, refusing to see anything funny in it.

"I'm not going to ask you again whether you're really going to marry this boy, Vary, all I'm going to say is, don't rush into anything. I meant what I said just now – he's a lightweight. You need a stronger man, someone who can—"

"Tame me?" Vary asked caustically.

Thorne shrugged. "Put it that way if you like. I wasn't going to. But you're a strong character yourself, you need someone who can match you."

"Dominate me, you mean. Someone who can subdue me, stop me from getting above myself." Vary stared at him, her brown eyes hostile. "Someone like you, for instance."

There was a moment of electric silence. Thorne's face changed abruptly, and Vary took a step back. Then he turned away.

"If you like to think so, yes," he said, and went into the cottage.

Any plans that might have been made for the following Sunday were thwarted when Zelah returned from the village with the news of a *pardon* that was being held in a town only a few miles away. Her face alight with pleasure, she begged Thorne to take another day off and attend. To Vary's surprise, he agreed.

"We've got on well with the work," he said. "I'd like to see this ceremony myself. They're quite a feature of Breton life, I believe. Have you ever seen one, Vary?"

"Yes, I have," Vary answered shortly. She'd been looking forward to going to this one with Gil, but only that afternoon he'd told her he wouldn't be able to see her on Sunday – "an old friend of my father", he'd explained apologetically. "He's heading south but stopping off near here for a weekend. I promised I'd spend the day with him, and it'd be too boring for you. So, we'll make it Monday, all right?"

She'd nodded, but now she was sorry. The prospect of a day without Gil was bleak. Still, she could have the cottage to herself. She wouldn't be having to avoid Thorne and Zelah.

But Zelah, it seemed, had other ideas. "You can come too," she offered. "You and Gil. We'll make a day of it, get to know each other better just as Gil suggested. What do you say?"

"I'm not seeing Gil on Sunday. He has to go and see a friend of his father's." And Zelah wouldn't want her to accompany them without Gil to keep her occupied, she thought. But here Zelah surprised her.

"Well, never mind. You can come. In fact, you'll have to – we can't leave you moping here all by yourself while we're having fun. Can we, Thorne?"

"Not if you say so," he returned, but his eyes were unfathomable. "Do you want to come with us, Vary?"

His tone was no more than polite. Clearly, he didn't want her along. Vary shook her head.

"No, I'd rather not. I'll stay here and—"

"You'll do no such thing!" Zelah gave her a warm smile and crossed to slip her arm through Vary's.

"Look, I know we started off badly," she went on persuasively, "but we can still be friends, can't we? You'll have to forgive me, I'm just a teeny bit jealous where Thorne's concerned, but can you blame me? And coming here to find you sharing this cottage with him – well! But I understand now. There could never have been anything between you and Thorne. And with you happily settled with Gil . . . let's start again, shall we? Come with us on Sunday and we'll have a wonderful day out and all be good friends."

Vary looked at her doubtfully. She didn't trust Zelah an inch, but was she being just a bit too suspicious? Zelah had done nothing to make her believe that there might be more behind this new overture than met the eye. She wasn't Vary's favourite kind of woman, it was true, but did that have to mean she was deliberately devious?

Vary glanced at Thorne, but there was nothing in his expression to guide her. She thought of going to the *pardon* with him. It might be their last day together. Even with Zelah there, wouldn't it be better than staying alone in the cottage? Even though any pleasure would be shot through with pain, wouldn't it be better to have that memory than a blank?

"All right," she said, "I'll come." And she gave Zelah a bright smile. Devious or not, she wasn't going to give her the satisfaction of seeing that she was suffering – not in any way.

And Vary kept to that determination during the whole

of the Sunday. They set off early in the morning, stopping on the way for lunch and arriving just in time to see the procession. Zelah was apparently delighted with everything: the crowds of excited French; the men and women in old Breton costumes; the candles, banners and statues of saints that were paraded round the streets. She produced a camera and took photograph after photograph, clinging to Thorne's arm in between and pointing out the things that pleased her most.

"Just look at that head-dress – isn't it delicious? Starched lace, wouldn't you say? So intricate. And the huge collar, it's simply gorgeous. I must have one – I could set a whole new trend!" She took several photos as the procession passed by, the men in embroidered waistcoats, the women's black dresses enlivened by satin and velvet in glowing colours. "Thorne, I am glad we came – aren't you, Vary?"

"Yes," Vary said, surprised to find that it was true. The bitter-sweetness of being with Thorne and Zelah was there, just as expected; but it had been alleviated by Thorne's attitude. For once, he seemed to have shed his cold, sardonic manner and become again the Thorne who had begun to emerge before Zelah's arrival. A warmth that she had almost forgotten was surfacing, and Vary realised that she had missed the humanity she knew to be there. If he weren't a humane, caring person, she thought, why would he be devoting himself to easing people's suffering? Why would he be turning his back on the possibilities of a lucrative private practice and spending his life amongst dirt and disease?

191

The procession passed slowly on, with a knot of pilgrims and priests chanting hymns and psalms, and a bishop with his brocaded robes and mitre. Vary watched as it wound its way through the ancient streets towards the church. These processions never failed to bring a lump to her throat; she swallowed, her eyes misting, and looked up to find Thorne watching her. That strange expression, the one she'd seen once or twice before, was on his face, but as soon as she caught his eye it vanished, to be replaced by his usual mask. But not quite, she thought. There was a lingering warmth there still, and she stood motionless unable to tear her eyes away, as the warmth deepened.

"Thorne! You're not listening," Zelah complained, and pulled at his arm. "There's going to be a fair next, in the old square. Can we go? I love fairs."

"It'll be quite ordinary," Thorne said. "Nothing unusual, except for the Breton wrestling which is rather like Cornish wrestling – there are a great many links between Brittany and Cornwall, as you know, even the place names are remarkably similar. But it'll probably be quite enjoyable. They play the bagpipes as well as accordions, and everyone lets their hair down. I don't mind stopping on for a while."

They wandered around the square, laughing at the sideshows, listening to the music and watching the wrestling and dancing displays. Vary began to feel that she had misjudged Zelah. Although still gushing possessively over Thorne, she was clearly setting out to be pleasant and had made none of her usual barbed comments. And Vary couldn't blame her for loving Thorne, it was just that she wasn't sure that the older woman did love him. But that was really Thorne's problem; there was nothing she could do about it.

It was late when they finally left the fair and turned the car towards home. Zelah sat in the front with Thorne, her head resting on his shoulder. Nobody said much. Vary, in the back, leant her head back and was suddenly assailed by loneliness. She'd been mad to come. She'd enjoyed the day, yes, Zelah had gone out of her way to make sure that she did. But to her dismay she found that she now loved Thorne even more deeply than before. And the consequent pain was all the more harsh.

Soon, she thought. Soon I'll leave and never see either Thorne or Zelah again.

Never seeing Zelah again was something she could tolerate. But never seeing Thorne again . . . ? The thought was almost unbearable.

"Well, that's it," Thorne remarked, turning the car into the narrow track. "A very pleasant day out. Thank you both. And tomorrow, it's back to work."

"But not for long," Zelah murmured. "We've nearly finished, and then we can have a *real* holiday. Can't we?"

But Vary didn't hear Thorne's reply. As the car drew to a halt she saw that the cottage door was wide open and a light shining on to the path. Jeff! she thought. Jeff's arrived early! And she leapt from the car and ran excitedly up the path.

"Jeff!" she called, barely aware that Thorne was close

behind her. "Jeff, you're here – how marvellous! Oh, Jeff, I've been longing to see you and talk to you. I . . ." Her voice died in her throat as she took in the door to the small bedroom standing wide open, the chaos inside the room, and the startled look on the face of the man who stood there. For a dizzy moment, her mind refused to recognise him, and then, bleakly, she knew the truth. "*Gil!*" she breathed, horrified. "Gil – what on earth are you doing?"

"It's all too clear what he's doing," Thorne said grimly, pushing past her. "He's trying to steal the formula and notes for the new drug. He's a spy, Vary, and you brought him here . . ."

Chapter Twelve

"A *spy!*"

Vary turned shocked eyes from Gil to Thorne. The world was swaying about her and she put out a hand for support. But Thorne, his eyes like burning stones, moved away.

"Don't play-act with me, Vary," he rasped. "I can only be taken so far for a ride, and you've managed to take me further than most. Wide-eyed innocence! I was right not to trust you, wasn't I? Right all along, though I tried not to believe it."

"Thorne, I don't know what you mean. I had no idea . . ." Vary turned back to Gil. "Gil, tell him I had nothing to do with this – with whatever you're doing." Her eyes moved about the room, taking in again the mess of papers, the signs of a frantic search. "What *are* you doing? What are you looking for? I don't understand."

"Don't you?" Thorne's voice was harsh. "Don't you really understand? Don't you know just what kind of a young man this is that you've taken up with? An opportunist, that's what he is – one who'll turn any situation to his own advantage, especially if there's money in it. You know very well I've been afraid of spies – that's why I looked for somewhere quiet, remote, where I could work without fear of intruders. That's why I asked Jeff if I could use this cottage. And that's why I didn't trust you when you first came, and why I should never have trusted you." Bitterness soured his tones. "My God, I'd never have thought I could be such a bad judge. Your big brown eyes really had me fooled there. And all the time, you were plotting with *him* – waiting until I'd almost finished before you carefully arranged for us all to be out so that he could come in and search at his leisure." He turned scathing eyes on Gil. "Unfortunately, you waited just a little too long. The relevant material isn't here. Zelah and I took the report and the formula to a colleague yesterday, and it's on its way to the proper authorities at this very minute. All that's left is my notes, and I doubt whether anyone would be able to decipher them, certainly not before the report's published."

Vary saw Gil shrug. "Story of my life," he said lightly. "Sorry for the mess, but I suppose it doesn't really matter. I might as well be on my way."

"Gil – you can't!" Vary took a step towards him, her eyes wide and imploring. "Gil, is it true? Was that really why you first spoke to me? So that you could find out about Thorne, so that you could steal his work? I can't believe it." Beseechingly, she gazed at him, and felt a chill as he smiled slightly.

"Well, what do you think? I had to get into the cottage

somehow, and there you were, all alone day after day . . . I couldn't pass up an opportunity like that, could I? You wouldn't expect me to. And don't say you didn't lap it all up, Vary. You were having the time of your life, let's face it. Being courted in that sweet, old-fashioned way – full moons, candlelit dinners, romantic picnics. And with all that hopeless love thrown in, what more could a girl ask? The yearning lover on the one hand, the broken heart on the other. It's something you'll remember for the rest of your life."

Vary stared at him. Could this really be the Gil who had begged her to marry him, who had declared that second-best would be enough? It had all been an act, a ploy to gain her confidence, to persuade her to let him into the cottage. She shook her head in hopeless negation.

"I never had any idea," she whispered. "You – you seemed so sincere. I was afraid of hurting you . . . And it was all a lie."

"Not quite all of it," he said. "I really did fancy you, Vary. Still do, as a matter of fact. So if you'd like to come with me – I can't really see you being welcome here any more – well, why not? We could go on with this trip of yours and have fun, just as we have done. We *do* have fun together, after all. You'd have to pay, of course, the story of my windfall wasn't true, unfortunately, and I was rather relying on the payment I'd be getting for this little job. Well, what d'you say?" He smiled disarmingly.

Vary gasped, but before she could speak Thorne cut

in. "All right, you two, break it up," he commanded. "You're not going to be travelling anywhere, Mitchell, unless it's to jail. You seem to forget that you've been caught in the act of committing a crime." He flicked Vary a brief, searing glance. "And I shouldn't be surprised if you go with him," he said coldly. "Accomplices are generally treated in the same way, I understand."

"But I'm not an accomplice! I had no idea. I never suspected for a moment." Vary turned from one to the other, her hands clenching convulsively, her eyes frantic. "Gil, tell him, *please*, that I didn't have anything to do with it – that I didn't know—"

Gil watched her reflectively. The pleasant openness had gone from his face, she saw despairingly, leaving it cold and calculating. He seemed to consider, then shook his head regretfully.

"I really don't think there's any point, do you? I mean, Thorne isn't going to believe a word I say, any more than he believes you. And you must admit it looks suspicious. They'll only have your word for it that we'd never met before – that it wasn't all planned. If I were to say you sent for me – well, they'd probably believe *that*. But to deny it – no, I don't think there's much chance, quite frankly."

Vary felt her body turn to ice. He was going to implicate her! He meant to tell the police that he'd known her before, that it had all been planned: her visit coinciding with Thorne's; her gaining his confidence; the subsequent meetings with Gil; and, finally, the day

198

out, giving Gil a chance to raid the cottage. None of it was true, but could she ever persuade them of that, if Gil refused to co-operate? Could she ever persuade Thorne?

If there had ever been any chance of Thorne's loving her, it had been killed now.

"You wouldn't do it," she said to Gil, knowing that he would, and without the slightest compunction. "You wouldn't really tell all those lies. Not after all you've said to me, not after all you've promised."

"Promises, promises," he answered lightly. "I don't think I've ever kept one in my life. That's not what they're *for*, Vary, my sweet. Not in my book, anyway. And I told you, I really do fancy you. It's been quite an achievement to act the modest swain. Not at all my style in the normal way."

Vary glanced helplessly at Thorne. Surely he could see that she was innocent, that Gil was playing her along? But there was a cynical twist to his lips as he watched, and her heart sank.

"I didn't know anything about it, Thorne," she said directly to him. "Please believe me. I had no idea."

"No? Perhaps you'll explain, then, why you decided to spend the day with Zelah and me, leaving the cottage free for him to explore? It was all very convenient, wasn't it? That tale about his having to meet a friend, so that you were at a loose end. And how you must have laughed when Zelah suggested that you should come with us, thus removing you – as you thought – from all suspicion. You must have taken me for a real fool, Vary. And maybe you were right, at that," he added bitterly. "That's exactly what I've been, as far as you were concerned – a real, blind fool."

It was no use. He would never believe her. Defeatedly, Vary turned away, away from both Thorne and Gil. The one whom she loved, and who could never love her; the other who had professed to love her, and had misused her emotions with a cruel calculation that appalled her.

I'll never love any man again, she thought bleakly. I'll never be able to trust enough.

As she turned away, she saw Zelah, still standing in the doorway, watching quietly. The blonde's face wore a curious expression, a mixture of triumph, delight and something that Vary couldn't at first recognise. It was something she had never seen on anyone's face before and it took her a moment or two to identify it. Then she realised – it was hate. But why should Zelah hate her? Vary was no threat to her plans. If she hadn't been sure of Thorne before, she must be now. It was inevitable that he would turn to her.

Zelah's eyes were fixed on Vary's face as she spoke. She knows just what I'm feeling, Vary thought, just what hell I'm going through. And she's pleased. *Pleased*. She tried not to listen to the older woman's words, but she couldn't close her ears.

"You're not going to prosecute Vary, are you, Thorne?" Zelah was saying in that husky voice. "I'm sure she never meant any harm. It's quite obvious, she was besotted by this young man and simply didn't realise what he was doing, or how serious it was. You can't really blame her."

"Vary knew exactly how serious it was," Thorne grated. "She helped me with the report, remember? I explained it all to her. There's no excuse."

"Well, but she's little more than a child," Zelah purred, crossing to Thorne's side. "Don't you see, she's had her punishment? Let her go, she isn't important. And then we'll decide what to do about Gil."

"I've already decided. Jail's too good, but it's all there is. I just hope he gets a long sentence."

"Oh, come." Gil sounded bored, and Vary turned to stare at him in fascination. How could he be so cool about it? "Look, I haven't committed any crime. I've been seen around with Vary for the past fortnight – anyone in the area will confirm that. Plenty of people know she's staying here – why shouldn't they believe she invited me, that I've had the run of the place? I've done no damage – lock-picking's one of my many accomplishments – and I've stolen nothing. Just what are you going to charge me with?" He examined his fingernails. "I don't even know what you're getting so het-up about. This drug formula, whatever it is – what does it matter who has it? It's going to be produced, it'll get to your precious India just the same. You may not have the glory of it all, but according to Vary, you're too altruistic to bother about that anyway. So where's the problem?"

"He's right," Zelah said into the silence. "There really isn't anything we can do about it, Thorne. And the formula's safe. So why don't we just let them both go and forget about it?" Her long, predatory fingers stroked his arm. "Forget it all, Thorne. Let's go back to England, or Paris. Why don't we have a few days in Paris? See the sights, have fun. You need a holiday, Thorne, not a lot of hassle over something that really doesn't matter." She leaned against him, pressing her body blatantly to his. "What do you say?"

Vary tore her eyes away. She didn't wait to hear what Thorne said. She made blindly for the doorway and ran out into the night. It was impossible to stay in that room a moment longer, with the man who hated her, the man who had betrayed her and the woman who was gloating over her humiliation. She wanted nothing else but to get as far away as possible.

Perhaps distance would lessen her agony. Perhaps time would perform its famous miracle of healing. Or perhaps neither would have any effect at all.

Whatever the truth, she couldn't stay there, to be humiliated by Zelah's condescension, to be seared by Thorne's contempt. She had to get away.

Dawn coloured the sky with shimmering mother-of-pearl, giving it the soft glow of the inside of an oyster-shell. The first birds sang, a faint breeze rustled the pliant stems of the tamarisk, and the scent of newly washed sand tingled in Vary's nostrils as she woke.

She stretched, stiff and uncomfortable. A grassy bank might be fine for lying on during the day, but it was cold and hard at night. And there had been nothing to wrap around her, nothing to keep the cool night air from chilling her skin.

Not that she would have felt any warmer if she had been wrapped in goose feathers, she thought bleakly as she stared at the sea. She had been chilled last night by more than the weather, and she doubted whether she would ever be truly warm again.

After her flight last night, there had been nowhere to go. The village was in darkness, everyone fast asleep and unaware of the drama taking place on their doorsteps. There had been no chance of any transport, and in any case she had no money, no papers, none of her belongings. She couldn't leave the cottage without them. So she had made for the beach, recalling inevitably that other time when she had fled here and Thorne had followed her, to reassure her that Zelah wasn't his wife, that she was still welcome. He hadn't followed her this time. He never would.

Had he let Gil go, as Zelah had suggested? Would he follow her other suggestion and leave the cottage, go to Paris for a few days and eat in those smart restaurants he had affected to despise, before taking Zelah back to England to marry her? Would he give up his research, his work in India, and take up some lucrative post – perhaps with Zelah's own father, or in private practice? Or perhaps he would concentrate now on his novels. Become a famous TV writer. There seemed no end to the opportunities open to Thorne.

Well, she would hear about him whatever he did. And she knew that each time she heard his name, saw an article about him in a paper or magazine, read one of his books or happened to catch sight of him on TV, she would suffer this same, exquisite pain all over again. There would be no escaping it.

At some time today, she would have to go back to the cottage to collect her things. She would wait until he had gone out – or gone away altogether. Seeing him again would be more than she could bear.

Chapter Thirteen

The hotel was at its busiest time, and full of guests. A coach party of Americans had just arrived and were standing about in the foyer, their luggage cluttering the floor, gazing around and remarking on the old oak beams, the panelled walls and ornately plastered ceiling. Vary sat at the reception desk, collecting passports, answering questions, noting down special requirements, with barely a moment to lift her eyes.

It had been like this ever since she'd arrived at the Falcon Hotel, close to one of England's most famous tourist centres. Their advertisement had certainly been right when it said the management was desperate – to be left without a head receptionist at the very beginning of the season was little short of a disaster. And to maintain their reputation as one of England's leading hotels, the manager had told her during their interview, they couldn't afford to employ anyone but the best. Vary had been relieved when her qualifications and references had convinced him that that was just what she was.

At least someone had faith in her, she thought as she switched from English to German for a family who had followed the coach party into the hotel. And during the eight weeks she had been working here, she'd done her best to justify that faith. All the same, her mind still tended to wander, during the few quiet moments of each day, to a small cottage on a quiet shore in Brittany. And at night, before she fell asleep from sheer exhaustion, it drifted inevitably to the picture of a lean, tanned face, dark hair and scorching blue eyes, lips that too often had a sardonic twist to them but could, on occasion, soften to a heart-melting tenderness.

"Yes," she answered automatically, "you can reach Stratford-on-Avon from here. It's a pleasant drive – I'll show you on the map. We've plenty of leaflets telling you what to see, and I can book seats at the Memorial Theatre for you." She smiled at the man who had asked, and then looked past him to the next guest.

It was Thorne.

Vary stood rock still. The noise of the foyer, the chatter and the laughter, faded away, leaving her in a vacuum of silence. Her eyes ceased to see the people who were still milling around, sorting out suitcases, queuing for the lift, going up and down the wide, carpeted staircase.

There were only she and Thorne in the whole world. Only his eyes, driving their powerful glance into her mind; only his lips, firm and unsmiling, only his presence, which could diminish the most impressive surroundings by the sheer force of his personality.

What had brought him here, to the very hotel where she was working? Why did fate have to be so cruel?

"Yes, sir," she said, dragging together all her shattered poise. "Did you wish to book a room?"

"I did." He was evidently going to play along with her, pretend they'd never met. She didn't know whether that hurt more or less; whether she wanted him to acknowledge her, with the inevitable scorn that would bring to his manner, or whether she preferred him to treat her as a stranger. "A large double, please, with a good view of the grounds and its own bathroom."

"All our rooms have their own bathroom, sir." A large double? So he wasn't alone. Presumably Zelah was with him, and she wondered if they were married yet. If they were, the press hadn't got hold of the story. Painfully, she acknowledged the fact that they might well be on their honeymoon.

She glanced quickly down the list. There was one room left, and she reached for the key and passed over the register. "I'll get someone to take up your luggage, sir."

"No need," Thorne said curtly, and he picked up the one suitcase that stood on the floor beside him and took the key. "Second floor? Is that the lift over there?" Vary nodded, watching him with puzzled eyes. Where was Zelah, and the luggage she would have brought with her? Vary couldn't imagine the exotic blonde putting her wardrobe into Thorne's small case. Perhaps she was coming later – in which case, they couldn't be on their honeymoon. But she still didn't know if they were married.

Thorne turned away without another word. The foyer was empty now, the new arrivals having at last made for their rooms, and Vary watched his tall figure stride across to the lifts. The shock of his sudden arrival was still making her heart thud, and her knees were weak. She was glad of the high stool on which she sat behind the reception desk.

"Wow!" the second receptionist remarked, and Vary turned to find that she too was watching Thorne. "What a gorgeous man! I didn't think they made them like that, outside of films."

"Oh, I don't know." Vary forced herself to speak casually. "I don't suppose he's any more special than anyone else, underneath the cheesecake."

"No?" The other girl gave her an amused glance. "That's not what your face was saying when he spoke to you! I got the impression you were distinctly smitten. Don't blame you, either. He can have the key to my room any time he likes!"

"Hazel, honestly!" Vary protested, but she couldn't help laughing. If you took Hazel seriously, you'd imagine she went to bed with a different man every night. In fact, as Vary knew, she was steadfastly faithful to her fiancé, the commis chef, and they were hoping to marry in a year or so and eventually run their own small hotel. "One of these days," Vary warned her, "someone's going to take you seriously."

"Oh, I know when to stop. But that man – he really is something else. He looked as if he was interested in you too, Vary."

"Rubbish!" Vary turned away to hide the crimson flags that she knew must be flying in her cheeks. Hazel was no fool and she'd spotted the communication between Thorne and Vary at once; it wouldn't take much for her to guess something very near the truth. "Anyway, I'm going off duty now," she added. "Stella's due on, isn't she? She can deal with the next coach." The switchboard light flashed and she lifted the receiver without noticing which room was calling. "Reception, can I help you?"

"I certainly hope so," a familiar voice grated in her ear. "When do you go off duty?"

"I—" Vary glanced around wildly. Hazel was talking to a guest about country parks, and Stella hadn't yet arrived. "I'm afraid I can't—"

"I don't want any excuses," Thorne interrupted. "I want to see you, Vary, and as soon as possible. I didn't chase half-way across Europe to be fobbed off now. You must be off soon. When can you come to my room?"

Never! Vary wanted to shout. I'm never coming to your room, or anywhere else where we might be alone. I don't want to see you again, don't you understand? That's why I ran away! But she couldn't say all that. Not here, with Hazel bright-eyed and curious by her side, and the foyer beginning to fill with guests again. She couldn't say anything that he would accept.

"I'm waiting, Vary," he said grimly. "I warn you, I mean to talk to you. If you won't come up here, I'll come down there. I don't especially want to wash all our dirty linen in the foyer of the Falcon Hotel, but if that's the way you want it . . ."

She knew that he meant it. "All right," she said faintly. "I'll come now." And she heard his satisfied grunt, before his receiver went down with a decisive click.

Vary put down her own receiver more slowly. Stella was behind the desk now, already looking through the registrations with a businesslike air. The man Hazel had been talking to had gone and she was now discussing the hotel kennels with a tweedy couple who had two labradors tying their leads into knots beside them. Vary gave Stella a brief résumé of the morning, and then went to fetch her jacket.

What could Thorne have to say to her? What did he mean about "chasing half-way across Europe"? Why had he come here at all?

She knew she would find out the answers when she went to his room, so why did she have this almost overpowering urge to run away again – to run anywhere, so long as Thorne Moran couldn't find her?

"So." Thorne opened the door to her knock, and looked down at her, grim and unsmiling. "I wondered if you would come."

"You didn't leave me a lot of choice." Vary went past him into the room, hearing him close the door behind her. A second click had her whirling round, just in time to see him remove the key from the lock.

"What are you doing? Why are you locking the door?"

"Because I don't want you to run away from me again." He came across the room, lithe as a panther, and stood a few inches away. Too close for comfort, she thought, as her heart began to slam against her ribs. "You've caused me enough trouble, Vary Carmichael," he went on. "I don't intend to take any more of it."

"So why seek me out? Why come after me? I've settled down here, I'm coping. Why stir everything up all over again?"

Thorne studied her. "You admit, then, that there is something to stir?"

Vary turned away. "I'm not admitting anything. Would there be any point? You didn't believe anything I told you the last time we were together."

Thorne was silent for a moment. Then she felt his hands on her shoulders. She stood perfectly still, fighting the sensations that surged through her at his touch; fighting the sudden desire to turn, to fling herself into his arms, find safety and love against his body. But there was no safety there, only dislike and contempt. No love, only hatred.

"Vary," Thorne said softly, and she stiffened at the new note in his voice. "Vary, listen to me. Turn and look at me. Please."

Please, he'd said. Slowly, Vary turned and looked up into his face, her eyes searching his. She couldn't afford to make any more mistakes. She had to be quite sure before she exposed herself to any more pain.

"Why did you come here, Thorne?" she asked quietly, and the shadows deepened in his eyes.

With a half-strangled groan, he caught her hard against him. The breath punched out of Vary's lungs, and her own arms went around him of their own accord. She clung tightly to him, her cheek pressed against the silkiness of his shirt, feeling the warmth of his skin and the steady beat of his heart. His arms were like iron around her, and she welcomed their ruthlessness. Just now, for as long as it might last, she wanted nothing else but this. To be held by Thorne as if he really wanted her, really loved her, to pretend for a while that it wasn't a matter of chemistry or lust, but something far deeper, far more real. To believe that they belonged to each other.

"Vary," Thorne said softly. "Do you really mean to say you don't know?"

"Know? What should I know?" She looked at him, still not daring to believe that this was really happening. "Don't tease me, Thorne. Don't make me guess. Don't you realise what it does to me – don't you realise what you've been doing to me all these months?"

"What *I've* been doing to *you*?" he said with a groan, and then caught her hard against him again. "Oh, Vary, my darling, my dear sweet darling, if only you knew . . . And you've been suffering too, I never intended that, never. Oh, my sweet, my *sweet* . . ."

"Thorne—" Still, she needed to hear the words. The closeness of him, the strength and hardness of him, the smell of his skin, the warmth of his hands and arms and body, all these threatened to overwhelm her. But she had been through too much uncertainty, too many sleepless nights, to be able to succumb so swiftly now. "Thorne—"

"I love you," he said, and his voice was as deep and dark as a cavern. "Vary, I love you. Don't you know that? Didn't you always know that?"

She closed her eyes and swayed against him. *I love you*. The words she had needed so desperately to hear echoed now in her mind, in her heart. And he thought she'd known. He'd thought she'd known!

"How could I know?" she asked. "You were like stone. How could I know what you were feeling?"

"Like stone?" He grimaced and shook his head. "Vary, I was melting inside the whole time. Even when I believed you were a spy – even at the very end when we caught that silly young fool burgling the cottage and I thought – well, never mind now what I thought – even then, I knew I was in love with you. I admit I tried quite hard not to be, to start with, but you got right under my skin, Vary, and there was no getting rid of you." His mouth twisted again, wryly. "I didn't even want to."

"Oh, Thorne—"

"And what about you?" he asked, with sudden urgency. "How do you feel about me, Vary? Sometimes I've thought you loved me too, but I've never really been sure. Tell me, for God's sake."

Vary stared at him in astonishment. "But of course I love you too! You ought to know that!" She caught his glance and smiled involuntarily. "Well, maybe I did try to hide it, but that was just because I was hurt, and because I didn't think there would ever be a chance. I had to try to make a life without you."

Thorne shook his head, a smile pulling at the corners of his mouth. "What a pair of fools we are." But his voice was gentle and his eyes warm as he looked down at her.

"Not any longer, though. We'll never try to hide from each other again."

Vary raised her face, lips parted for the kiss she knew must come. It was as tender as an April sky, as soft as a summer breeze, and it swept through her heart, washing away all the unhappiness, the frustration and the desolation that she'd been feeling for the past months. Confident now, she returned the kiss, adding a sweetness of her own. Thorne was hers, always had been and always would be.

At last he raised his head, parting reluctantly from her lips. He looked down at her and brought one hand up to trace with a fingertip the line of her brow, the soft curve of her cheek, the tender fullness of her lips.

"You've lost weight, Vary," he said. "You're as slim as a reed. What happened to you when you ran away?"

Vary shrugged. "I spent the night on the beach. I didn't have anywhere else to go. I waited until you left the cottage with Zelah, and then I collected my things and left a letter for Jeff, telling him I couldn't wait. I hated doing that, but I simply couldn't face any more. And I knew he'd understand. And then I just went on."

"But you didn't continue with your trip. I tried every way I knew to find you. Jeff had some idea of your itinerary, but there was never any sign of you. It didn't make sense."

"I gave it up," she confessed. "I didn't have any heart to go on. I came back to England and got this job here."

"I knew something had happened, but Jeff wouldn't tell me. He said you'd made him promise." A smile quirked his mouth. "You didn't make him promise not to hint, though. In the end, he took pity on me and gave me a kind of riddle to solve, and it led me here."

"I'll have something to say to Jeff when I see him again," Vary vowed. Then she, too, smiled. "Like – thank you!"

They sat quietly together for a while, neither of them wanting to break the spell by going too fast. Then Thorne spoke again, his voice as caressing as brown velvet, as she had known from the start it must be.

"I nearly went mad that night, after you'd run away," he said. "I just didn't know what to believe. I knew I loved you, I'd known that for a long time. But who was it I loved? A real, flesh-and-blood Vary who could be obstinate and funny and sweet and infuriating? Or a cardboard character, with a two-faced, devious little bitch living behind the façade? I knew what I wanted to believe, but was I crazy? I just didn't know."

He stroked her hair absently, his mind back in that tiny cottage on a warm Sunday evening. "It was obvious what Gil was – a weak young opportunist who'd grab any chance of making some easy money. But had he deceived you, or were you really conniving with him? I just couldn't tell and it nearly drove me mad. And then you ran away. And everything changed."

"Changed? How?"

"You haven't seen me in a real temper yet," he said grimly. "You may think you have, but that night I surprised even myself. Both Gil and Zelah were terrified, they must have thought I was going to run amok with a hatchet, I think! Anyway, they came across with the truth. The real truth."

"*Zelah*? You mean – *she* was in it?"

"Up to her neck," he nodded. "Not from the beginning, and not for financial gain. No, she just wanted to get rid of you. She wanted me, as you must have noticed, and she was determined to get me."

"I thought you wanted her too," Vary murmured, and he shook his head.

"No. I allowed her to give you that impression –" he looked slightly shamefaced "—but there was never anything in it, as far as I was concerned. I just wanted to make you jealous, I suppose. There was Gil – I didn't seem able to do anything about that. And there was Jeff."

"*Jeff*?"

"Yes. Sounds idiotic now, I know, but you talked of him with such affection, I really thought there must be something between you. Jeff soon put me right about that, once he'd eventually arrived and I could talk to him. Did you know he's hoping to get married soon?"

"No!" Vary sat bolt upright. "And he never told me! Who is she? Has he known her long? Do I know her?"

"I don't know. I don't know anything about her! And I was trying to tell you about Zelah." Thorne shook her gently. "Be quiet, woman, and listen."

"Sorry." Vary snuggled against him again. Somehow she didn't feel very interested in Zelah any more. Thorne didn't love her, he wasn't going to marry her, that was all that mattered. "Tell me, then."

"Well, Zelah knew about my fears that someone was spying on me, trying to get details of the new drug. She guessed it was Gil as soon as she saw him, they recognised the same ruthless streak in each other, I suppose. That afternoon, when we found you in the garden, Zelah went to the village, remember? She followed Gil to his *auberge* and they talked. And made their plans for the following Sunday."

"So it was all a set-up job," Vary breathed, and he nodded.

"Zelah got you and me out of the way and left the cottage free for Gil to move in. Unfortunately for Gil, Zelah was using him for her own purposes – to stir up trouble for you. She told him we wouldn't be back until much later. So we caught him red-handed, just as Zelah had intended us to."

"Poor Gil," Vary said. "He won't make a very good criminal."

"I don't think he'll make a criminal at all. I didn't prosecute him after all – as he pointed out himself, there was nothing really to charge him with and he hadn't done any actual harm. I just sent him on his way. I suppose he'll live on his wits for a while and then get himself some sort of job. Probably spend his life operating just inside the law."

"And Zelah?"

"I sent her on her way as well, the next morning. That's when you saw us going out." His arms tightened around her. "If I'd only known you were so near, on the beach . . . Didn't you realise I loved you?"

Vary shook her head. "You hid it well. Oh, Thorne – make me realise now. Love me – please."

His eyes gleamed. "Before the white wedding, with all the frills? Or would you really hate that kind of wedding?"

"I don't mind what sort I have," Vary said softly, "as long as you're there. And as long as it's soon. But meanwhile – love me, Thorne. I want to belong to you. I've waited so long."

"And so have I." He touched her cheek softly, and then let his fingers slip down into the neck of her blouse. "I think we've both waited long enough." His lips touched hers, tender yet with a tautness that betrayed the deep passion beneath. "Vary – there's just one more thing I have to know. Will you come to India with me?"

"I was thinking of going anyway," she told him. "Without you, if I had to. Yes, I'll come. I'll work beside you. And I'll learn all the new languages I need to be of some use."

"You'll be of use anyway," he told her just before their passion swept away all need to talk. "You'll be there for everyone to love. But especially me."

The late afternoon sunlight flooded the room with golden colour. And Vary released the last of her doubts and gave herself wholeheartedly to the man who had held her heart ever since she had first set eyes on him. The firestorm could, at last, be allowed to burn unchecked.